www.randomhousechildrens.co.uk

donuts

THE DONUT DIARIES

ESCAPE FROM CAMP FATSO

THE DONUT DIARIES

of Dermot Milligan

ESCAPE FROM CAMP FATSO

As told by Anthony McGowan
Illustrated by David Tazzyman

CORGI

THE DONUT DIARIES: ESCAPE FROM CAMP FATSO
A CORGI BOOK 978 0 552 56440 3

Published in Great Britain by Corgi Books,
an imprint of Random House Children's Publishers UK
A Random House Group Company

This edition published 2012

1 3 5 7 9 10 8 6 4 2

The Random House Group Limited supports The Forest Stewardship Council (FSC®), the
leading international forest certification organization. Our books carrying the FSC label
are printed on FSC®-certified paper. FSC is the only forest certification scheme endorsed
by the leading environmental organizations, including Greenpeace. Our paper procurement
policy can be found at www.randomhouse.co.uk/environment.

Set in Bembo Regular 13pt/22pt

Corgi Books are published by Random House Children's Publishers UK,
61–63 Uxbridge Road, London W5 5SA

www.**randomhousechildrens**.co.uk
www.**totallyrandombooks**.co.uk
www.**randomhouse**.co.uk

Addresses for companies within The Random House Group Limited can be found at:
www.randomhouse.co.uk/offices.htm

THE RANDOM HOUSE GROUP Limited Reg. No. 954009

A CIP catalogue record for this book is available from the British Library.

Printed and bound by CPI Group (UK) Ltd, Croydon, CR0 4YY

To the illustrative genius of David Tazzyman;

and to Andy Stanton, who raised the bar,

leaped it, and then made rude gestures

from the far side to try to put me off.

Friday 30 March

'Cheer up, Donut,' said Renfrew, a happy smile on his goofy face.

Normally he looked a lot like a vole, but today, for some reason, I thought he had moved more in the direction of squirrel.

Or possibly gerbil.

'No,' I replied.

We were walking towards the school gates on our way home. It was the last day of term, and the two-week-long Easter holiday lay ahead.

THE LAST DAY OF TERM!!!!!

Throughout history, human kids have marked the end of term with grand celebrations. In the Stone Age they would paint themselves blue and dance naked around a roasting mammoth. The Romans used to hold massive end-of-term gladiatorial contests, where the guy with a net and a trident and a really short skirt would fight some other guy with less cool but probably more efficient weapons and a slightly longer skirt, while the kids yelled encouragement and feasted on larks' tongues and fried bats. In the Middle Ages, nerdy children would clutch ribbons and skip around a giant stick while the cool kids jeered and hurled rocks at them.

Yes, it should have been a great day.

So how come I looked like someone who'd had all the jam sucked out of his last donut, to be replaced by some other disgusting slop, such as monkey poo or cat sick?

The answer lay in two words. Two fatal, deadly, foul, evil, putrid, stinking words.

CAMP. FATSO.*

'It's your own fault, really,' said Spam, my second best friend.

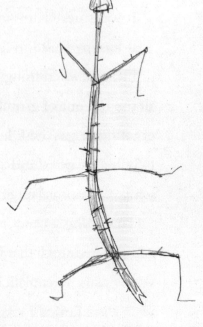

---

* Camp Fatso is basically a place where fat and/or generally unhealthy kids are sent to be made thinner and/or healthier, by means of cross-country runs and gruel.

If Renfrew, my first best friend, was a vole (or squirrel or gerbil), then Spam was a stick insect that had been zapped up to giant size in a freak nuclear accident.

It was true.

It *was* my fault.

I hate it when things are my fault. It takes all the fun out of grumbling. But there it was, pointing at me, the Obese Finger of Truth. I couldn't avoid the fact that I had sort of semi-volunteered to go to Camp Fatso.

This was as a result of a) a really, really complicated story that would take me another whole diary to explain,* and b) realizing that I

* OK, OK, let's just say that it involved some chimpanzee poo, a plot to frame me, an elaborate counter-plot and, well, lots more poo. Pretty disgusting, really. You can read all about it in the second volume of my memoirs, *The Donut Diaries: Revenge Is Sweet*.

was, in fact, a little too plump, on account of my donut addiction, and could actually do with a bit of slimming down.

And so I responded to Spam's statement in time-honoured fashion: by hitting him with my school bag and calling him a stupid lanky streak of camel pee.

Even without the looming horror of Camp Fatso it had been quite a traumatic last day of term. Nothing bad happened for the first half of it, if you exclude the fact that the last school dinner was some sort of pie that should have been standing trial at the International War Crimes court in The Hague. So obscurely disgusting was this pie that not even the dinner ladies could tell us what sort of pie it was. Spam hazarded a guess at hedgehog.

Personally, I thought it might have been whale and bacon.

Either way, it was no sort of preparation for the absolute and utter final last lesson of term, which was PE. I suppose I should have had an inkling of what was coming. Mr Fricker, our deeply demented PE teacher, was famous for two things:

1. The variety of screw-on mechanical contraptions which appeared in place of actual human hands;

2. His last-day-of-term football matches, which often had a casualty list exceeded only by a few famous battles, such as the Somme and Stalingrad.

And so, for the last lesson of term, Mr Fricker warmed us up by shouting at us for a while about personal hygiene (one of his obsessions), going into embarrassing detail about which parts of our bodies we should wash most thoroughly, and which bits shouldn't be washed at all, except under qualified medical supervision.

And then it was out onto the field for a classic David vs Goliath contest, with my form, Burton (David), taking on the might of Xavier (Goliath).

Just to explain, our school has four forms: Burton, which has all the duffers, fatties and weirdos; Campion, which is for the brainiacs; Newman, which is for the sporty-but-thick types; and Xavier, which has the kids who are good at everything, except being decent human beings.

We have PE lessons with Xavier, about half of whom are in the school football team, including my mortal enemy, the

Floppy-Haired Kid.*

No one from Burton is in any of the school teams, not even for games like ping-pong and badminton, designed for people who aren't very sporty or co-ordinated. Most of us are useless, although my friend Corky is quite dangerous. I don't mean dangerous as in a dangerous striker who might inflict damage on the opposing defence. I mean dangerous in that he might well crash into you at high speed, and then try to chew your knee-caps off.

Renfrew and Spam, needless to say, were so incompetent that if you watched them in isolation you just couldn't guess what sport they

* The Floppy-Haired Kid, or FHK for short, or Really Nasty Sly Spiteful Rotten Sneak for long, was the one who tried to frame me with the poo, as mentioned above. He failed because of my genius for counter-plotting.

were playing. Instead of football it could easily be golf, or even the ancient Icelandic pastime of Falling Over For No Good Reason At All.

I was actually one of our better players, which tells you all you need to know.

'And to add a bit of spice to the occasion,' Mr Fricker decreed in one of his less shouty voices (although by any normal standards he was screaming), 'the losers will clean the boots of the winners. And,' he added, 'I'll even things up by playing for the Xaviers.'

'But we've already got eleven, sir,' said Justyn Bragg, who hadn't quite got it yet.

'I'm afraid you're injured,' said Fricker, his stare suddenly as cold as a nudist on a glacier drinking a glass of liquid nitrogen.

'But I'm not injured,' said Justyn, still not getting it.

'Not injured *yet*,' said Fricker, screwing in his football hands, which were basically the same as his punching-a-rabbit-to-death hands, at which point Bragg got it, and started limping extravagantly.

Outside, the rain had begun to turn into sleet, as it usually did for outdoor PE. The pitch was made up almost exclusively of mud and puddles. I saw a solitary blade of grass, standing there like the sole survivor of some terrible disaster that had wiped out all other plant life from the earth.

'This is going to be fun,' said Renfrew.

'No, it isn't,' said Spam, who had a way of missing sarcasm, even when it reached up and slapped him in the face. 'I think it's going to be really unpleasant.'

And how right he was.

We Burtons were playing into the wind in the first half, and most of the team huddled together like sheep, while the Xaviers streamed through us like the marauding Mongol warriors of Genghis Khan.

I'm sure I don't need to tell you who played the part of Genghis.

Mr Fricker was all over the pitch, yelling out commands, screaming for the ball, crunching into tackles, chopping down his enemies with his mighty sword. Well, not the sword part. But anyone who got in his way would end up face-down in the mud, with the imprint of Fricker's football studs on the back of his neck.

By this stage the girls had finished their netball match and had come over to watch us. This added greatly to the embarrassment.

The basic rule in life is that when you're being humiliated it's best not to also have a load of girls laughing at you and yelling out, 'Hey, fatty, shift yourself, we can't see what's happening!' and, 'He doesn't know where he's going, he needs a fat-nav!' and that sort of thing.

I particularly didn't like being watched by the girl known as Tamara Bello (because that was her name), who didn't bother yelling insults, but just looked vaguely bored by it all, as if she'd rather be reading her book of short stories by Chekhov, a Russian author who died in prison, where he'd been sent for murdering millions of people by boredom.

And then, on the field, farce turned to tragedy, as it so often does. Or maybe this was more tragedy turning to farce. No, actually, this was farce turning into even bigger farce.

We were six–nil down. The Floppy-Haired Kid had scored two goals, and Fricker had smashed in the other four. We were just generally praying for it all to be over so that we could get down to cleaning the boots of the sneering Xaviers, and then going home to lick our wounds, eat our donuts, etc., etc.

Then the FHK got the ball and went for his hat trick. I tried to tackle him, but he dribbled round me, stopped, ran back and dribbled round me again, smirking all the time. I got rather annoyed about that, as it was adding insult to injury, and adding insult to injury is pretty bad, being beaten for unpleasantness only by adding another injury to the first injury.

So I was a bit riled. I chased after the FHK as best I could. I wouldn't normally have much chance of catching him, but I had a lucky break –

the ball hit a giant puddle and floated away, out of his control. Suddenly there were a load of us splashing around in there like, oh, I don't know, otters or seals or something, which was quite good fun.

The FHK was enjoying it rather less than the rest of us because he didn't like getting dirty or having his hair messed up, so he tried to deliver one of his sly and nasty kicks in the general direction of my rear end, but he only succeeded in slipping and getting a mouthful of muddy water.

The ball broke loose, and I was the one nearest to it. Most of the players were caught up in the massive puddle-splashing fight, and I realized that I had a chance to trundle up the pitch and score a consolation goal.

Mr Fricker, however, had other ideas.

Consolation goals were not part of his world view. He believed that you haven't really beaten your opponent until you've ground him into the dirt. 'The point,' he said to us once, 'is not to defeat the opposition, but to DESTROY IT.'

So as I ran with the ball up towards the other end of the pitch, with the girls laughing at my chubby white legs and my own team more interested in the mud fight, I sensed the oncoming approach of the insane PE teacher. His fist-shaped football hands were pumping up and down like the pistons of a nightmare express train powered by rocket fuel and high-octane fart gas.

He could probably have just tackled me, but he wanted more than that. He wanted to get across the message that nobody scores against the Fricker. In fact, nobody should even try.

So he launched himself into one of his infamous sliding tackles, otherwise known as 'the Scythe', the purpose of which is to crunch through your legs like a hatchet through dry sticks. I prepared for the agony, expecting to spend some time flying through the air before landing on my head. There was a small chance that Fricker's tackle would actually kill me, and I imagined all the nice things people would say about me at my funeral service, although it was sort of ruined by the presence of Ruby and Ella, my horrible sisters, who didn't take it seriously at all and laughed and chewed gum through the whole thing and turned it into a Fiasco.

But death for Dermot did not result, on this occasion. Mr Fricker began the sliding part of the tackle. He was about ten metres away when he initiated the Scythe. To begin with it all went well. Fricker was horizontal, and heading straight for my legs, cutting through the mud and surface water like a powerboat. I saw the metal of his football studs gleaming – the rumour was that he sharpened them to improve their grip and cutting edge. They were like the slashing claws on the back legs of a velociraptor.

I seriously considered screaming, but decided against it because of Tamara Bello. The same went for wetting my pants. I didn't know much about girls, but I did know that screaming and pant-wetting are quite far down the list of ways to impress them, coming just above bad breath and just below following through after a wet fart.

And then I noticed the look on Fricker's face. At the beginning of his slide it had been his standard, steely, children-slaughtering look. And then it changed, first to a look of mild surprise,

then horror, and finally agony. He was still sliding, but his speed was slowing. I realized that he wasn't actually going to reach me. The whole thing had been initiated too early, so desperate was Fricker to chop my legs off before I had the chance to score. But I still couldn't quite work out why his face was purple and his eyes were crossed.

Finally he came to a complete stop. There was the PE teacher, lying on his back in the mud, staring up at the sky and emitting the sort of sound you'd expect from a wounded bat.

'You OK, sir?' I said, walking towards him tentatively. Approaching injured PE teachers is one of those things, like going back to a lit firework you think has gone out, or plucking a bum hair from a sleeping buffalo, that is definitely not recommended. A few other kids had come up by now.

'His shorts,' said someone. 'Look at his shorts.'

Generally, most of us tried to avoid looking at Mr Fricker's shorts, but once my gaze was directed there I understood immediately what had happened. Mr Fricker's long slide had resulted in his shorts getting rammed right up his . . . I mean into his . . . Well, let's just say that he'd given himself the mother of all wedgies. And now he was clawing at the shorts with his artificial hands. But the trouble was that, as I've said, he had his punching hands on, which were clearly totally useless at pulling shorts out of bum cracks. It was kind of tragic. Someone behind me said something in a low voice, and someone else spluttered. I looked around. I saw the smirking face of the FHK. He was enjoying the spectacle. Up until then, something inside me, something horrible and mean-spirited, had been enjoying it too. But I realized that anything that amused the FHK couldn't really be funny.

'We can't leave him like this,' said Renfrew, who was now at my side, as he usually was at times of crisis.

'What can we do?' I said.

'You're going to have to go in,' said Spam, looming up on my other flank, as he also usually did when I needed him, or when we were just hanging out, getting chips, sitting on walls, etc., etc.

'Why me?' I asked, but only in the way every hero at some point or other in the story tries to Escape His Destiny. I already knew the answer. It was because I was standing a bit closer to Fricker than everyone else, and so it was, by the iron laws of schoolboy logic, up to me.

I nodded.

'OK, Renfrew, give me your sock.'

'My sock?'

'Just get on with it, man, there's no time to lose.'

'B-but—'

'NOW!'

Fricker had now gone from purple to white. Blood circulation had clearly been impeded, if not cut off altogether.

I held out my hand, and Renfrew laid a muddy sock in it. I kneeled beside the PE teacher.

'Can you hear me, sir?' I said.

Fricker blinked a couple of times. I think his sight may have gone. A dry tongue flicked at his lips.

'I'm going to try to yank them out, sir. The shorts, I mean. It's going to hurt. You should bite on this.'

I put Renfrew's sock between the parched

lips, and Fricker clamped down on it. And
then, amid the horrified groans of the crowd,
which now included the girls and their netball
teacher, Miss Gunasekara, I heaved at the small
amount of short fabric that was still visible. Mr
Fricker became utterly rigid, as if he'd been
given an electric shock. To begin with there
was no movement from the shorts: they were
so embedded I thought only dynamite would
extract them. Then I felt a tiny tremor. They
were shifting! But it was all proving too much
for me. I was already worn out from the football.
Sweat poured into my eyes. My muscles shook
and I could feel the cold talons of cramp begin to
pierce my biceps.

Fricker was staring at me now, although I
don't know what he was actually seeing. Perhaps
rather than the overweight kid before him, he

saw the gates of heaven, or an open football goal, or the mother and father who'd abandoned him as a child.★

Anyway, he was losing his grip on life, as I was losing my grip on his shorts. And then I felt a pair of immensely powerful hands close around mine, and smelled, at the same moment, a strong whiff of horse meat.

It was Ludmilla Pfumpf, the strongest and most fearsome human being in our year.★

★ I should say that I've no idea if he really *was* abandoned as a child, but nor do I know for certain that he wasn't, so it's definitely within the realm of possibility, and would explain a lot.

★ In fact, Ludmilla is probably one of the top ten most fearsome creatures in any year of any school, if you exclude the Beelzebub School for Demons, Devils and Monsters, in Hades itself. She was also wrapped up in the events of last term. She's basically a kindly ogress who keeps her chips in her armpit. She had a gigantic crush on the FHK, and part of my brilliant counter-plot involved me getting them together for snogging purposes, hehehe!

Together we made one last, supreme effort, and with a noise like the roar of a military jet passing over our heads, Mr Fricker's shorts were torn from his bottom.

Immediately, Miss Gunasekara, who'd been paralysed by fear or fascination throughout the whole operation, went into action. She took a netball bib from one of the girls and covered Mr Fricker's shame, and then yelled at us all to go back to the gym and get changed.

None of the kids thanked me for rescuing Fricker, and in fact most of them, led by the FHK, called me various names, the mildest of which was teacher's pet. It wasn't surprising, really. He was a dangerous lunatic, and we'd all have been safer if he'd been permanently disabled by the Epic Wedgie.

But I didn't mind. I knew I'd done the right thing.

And now the day was done, and we were going home.

I looked at Renfrew and Spam.

'Donuts on me, gentlemen,' I said.

After what I'd just seen and done, I certainly needed a few.

DONUT COUNT:

Well, I needed something to erase the image of Mr Fricker's auto-wedgie from my mind.

Saturday 31 March

10 a.m.

Right, my scheme for today is to hit town for a last taste of freedom before my stomach is imprisoned in the Inhuman Conditions of Camp Fatso on Monday, for two terrible weeks.

I'd watched the Camp Fatso promotional DVD with my parents, and it was scary stuff. Healthy food, cross-country runs, no mobiles or computers. In other words, every adult's idea of what kids should be doing, and every kid's idea of hell.

My plan for today – and I believe that it is a classic – is to sample every single forbidden food, all the evil, fat-drenched, sugar-coated, high-calorie, nutrient-low nasties that Camp Fatso was designed to exclude.

There's nothing fancy-nancy about my targets. This isn't the time for exquisitely arranged plates adorned by tiny sculptures made from whittled radishes.

I am going for the Magnificent Seven:

1. Cheeseburger
2. Kentucky Fried Chicken
3. Meat-feast pizza (with quite literally ALL THE MEATS, from aardvark to zebra, by way of spider monkey, camel and tapir)

4. Kebab (from the awesome King Kong Kebab Shop next to the bus station)
5. Ice-cream sundae (at least as big as my head)

And finally, the crowning glory – my new favourite donut:

6. The Butterscotch Explosion: a donut injected with a filling of soft caramel, with broken crystallized sugar sprinkled on the top, and melted toffee drizzled over the sugar.

Ah, only six, you say. But I plan to buy *two* donuts!

And I know you're thinking that it's nuts to passively accept my Camp Fatso sentence in the hopes of actually shedding a few belly-scoops of flab, and then go on such a monstrous eating binge. Doesn't that undermine exactly what I am trying to achieve? Aren't I biting off my nose to spite my face – biting it off, that is, sprinkling it with bacon bits and icing sugar, frying it in lard and then covering it in melted chocolate and eating it?

No.

Not in the least. That's where we come to part two of my plan, which is to take exactly one bite (or slurp, or lick, as appropriate) from each of these foody delights. No more, no less. Altogether this will add up to one reasonably large, but not insanely HUGE, meal.

And I'm using quite a lot of psychology here. I've found that a big part of the enjoyment of eating is in the anticipation –

you see that lovely mound of food in front of you, and you eat it in your mind before you put it in your mouth. And isn't that first bite always the best? And doesn't it always go a bit downhill after that?*

Your next question is probably going to be, given that I only have twelve pounds saved up, how am I going to pay for all that food, most of which will be wasted?

This is where part three of my plan comes into operation.

It brilliantly utilizes my dad's manky toenail.

I've got this theory that nearly all dads have a manky toenail. It just goes with being a dad,

* Let's say the first mouthful scores a maximum ten, the next will be a nine, then an eight, and so on. Not that it ever reaches a zero, not unless you're talking vegetables. But then vegetables begin at zero, so it's not saying much.

along with forgetting where you've put your keys and not listening when ladies tell you about what sort of day they've had. You should probably check your own dad's feet, just to see.

Anyway, my dad got his manky toenail from playing five-a-side football, which he does every Wednesday night. Playing five-a-side football is basically the only way to get him out of the toilet, where he mostly lives. He used to be good at football when he was at school, and I think he's probably still not bad, although it helps that he plays with a load of old codgers just as wrecked as himself.

The manky toenail arrived on the scene a couple of months ago. Dad came home after a game limping like he'd been shot in the leg with a bazooka. Well, OK, probably not a bazooka, as that would have completely blown his leg off, and one of the rules about having your leg blown off is that you get around by hopping rather than limping. Unless you've had an artificial leg fitted, but there wasn't time for that. So in he came, moaning and generally making a fuss, with his face all drained of colour like there'd been a terrible tragedy – which, in a way, if you were one of his toes, would be true.

It was one of the few evenings when we were all at home together – that's me, my mediumly-scary-but-also-quite-nice mum, my goth sister, Ella, and my pink sister, Ruby. In the evenings, Ella is generally to be found hanging around the graveyard with the other members of the Undead Community, and Ruby's usually doing pink things with her pink friends in her pink bedroom.

Anyway, like I said, we were all there for a change, and we were staring at my dad's feet, as there was nothing on the telly.

We'd all gathered round while he took his trainers off, and then shrank back in horror when we saw the blood soaking through the toe-end of his sock. My mum peeled the sock off while my dad pretended to be brave. What was underneath was really quite disgusting. The big toenail on his right foot was hanging by a thread. Well, not really a thread, more a strand of nail. It had broken right at the base, and there was toe-blood (definitely one of the worst kinds of blood) everywhere.

My mum's not usually very sympathetic about my dad's various ailments and complaints, such as his hay fever, his backache, the mysterious ringing in his ears and his periodically itchy bottom, but even she was shocked into sympathy. She gave him a wooden hairbrush to bite down on while she used the kitchen tongs to pull off the destroyed nail.

My dad made a noise like a dying buffalo. Ella did a sort of fainting thing that I'm pretty sure used to be called a 'swoon' in the olden days, and Ruby threw up into the fruit bowl.

Her sick was pink, which in itself raised all kinds of questions, but we can't go into that now.

The point of all this is that my dad's severed big toenail has lived on our kitchen windowsill ever since that evening. Over the months the

toenail

blood turned a deep purply-black, and the nail itself buckled and thickened till it looked like a fossilized claw. If you were ever going to have nightmares about a toenail, then this is the nail you'd be dreaming of.

I don't really know why it stayed on our kitchen windowsill for so long. It could just be that nobody wanted to touch it, or maybe it had become invisible, the way some old ornaments that have been in the same place for ever become invisible.

But I've now found the perfect use for it. This is the most brilliant part of my plan. You see, what I intend to do is this: at each café, restaurant, etc., etc. I will order my food, ravish the plate with my eyes, take a good big bite, savour the flavour, roll it around in my mouth, and swallow. I will then plant the manky toenail on the plate, and make a serious but dignified complaint. Everyone will be totally disgusted and freaked out by the toenail, and I'll be able to leave without paying, carefully taking the toenail with me, so that I can repeat the trick at the next eatery.

One of the many beauties of this scheme is that no one will think it's a scam, because I'll only have had one bite. And who would leave a meal after one bite, unless they really did find a blackened toenail in their cheeseburger?

Genius, see.

And now it's time to go and put it into operation. I shall report back in due course.

Saturday 31 March

8 p.m.

Why must all my dreams of glory end like this,
in defeat and disgrace?

It says in a book somewhere (don't ask me
which one, I've read several): 'Those whom the
gods love die young.'

Well, there should be another saying: 'Those
whom the gods hate they first make a bit fat and
then heap humiliation on their heads.'

Truly the gods must hate me.

All went quite well, to begin with. I dressed in my baggiest trousers to accommodate any slight expansion in the gut area that might arise from my expedition. I got the bus into town, and it was one of the most delightful bus journeys I've ever taken, purely because of what I said earlier about anticipation being the best part of eating.

The first thing that went wrong occurred as I took a short cut along a narrow alleyway connecting two streets, one of which held the gleaming temple of joy that would provide the Sacred Cheeseburger. There was just enough room for two people to pass each other. It was actually a pretty good place for a mugger to hang out, but I reckoned I was pretty safe at twelve o'clock on a Saturday afternoon. Plus, I had the world's uncoolest mobile. It was an old pink Crapia, discarded by Ruby, that I'd painted battleship grey using my model aircraft paint. I kept this well hidden from prying eyes, i.e. any of my mates or anyone else who might know me. But if there was a mugger, then I'd happily give them a tenner to take it off my hands.

For some reason I decided to check my money halfway along the alleyway. I'd raided my money box, so I had a ton of change, and I just wanted to make sure there was enough to start the giant food-ball rolling. I scooped a load out of my pocket, but a few coins spilled out onto the grimy floor of the alley. I knelt down to pick it up, and at the same moment heard a giggling, chattering, empty noise that could mean only one thing. A very bad thing. A gang of girls was approaching.

I suddenly felt really silly, scrabbling around

after coppers and five-pence pieces. But I also thought it would look like I was trying to be flash if I just got up and left it all there. You know, *Oh, look at me, I'm so posh I can just leave money lying on the ground, lah-di-dah, lah-di-dah, I'm just going to put on a silk dressing gown and do a little bit of ballet.*

It was an actual, authentic dilemma, like in a movie where the hero has to decide, say, whether to save his girlfriend from the jaws of a crocodile or to rescue a small child who's about to totter over the edge of a volcano into the fiery, bubbling lava below. Obviously, in the movie he'd end up doing both, probably using the stunned crocodile to catch the kid or something, but this wasn't a movie. This was the thing that scientists have calculated is 87.4 per cent worse than movies: this was Real Life.

So, not feeling too happy, I glanced up. And I found myself staring right into the dark eyes of Tamara Bello. She gave me this look that said, *What the heck are you doing here, scrabbling about on the dirty floor, blocking the way of me and my posse?* There was also a supplementary question that asked, *Just what sort of a buffoon are you, anyway?*

Then her face changed to something slightly different.

An expression for which the word 'revulsion' may well have been invented.

All the time I'd been vaguely picking up my coins without paying proper attention to what I was doing. Now I looked down and saw that what I'd thought was a coin was in fact a piece of squashed chewing gum, and my fingers were halfway through the act of prying it off the floor.

'Look at that fat kid scraping gum off the

floor!' screeched one of the girls, who was dressed up as if she was going clubbing, even though it wasn't anywhere near disco o'clock. She wasn't from my school. Nor were the others, apart from Tamara, and she obviously wasn't going to admit that she even knew me.

'Have a fresh one,' Tamara said, and dropped a piece of gum next to me as she and the others skipped past. One of them stepped on my hand, and another stuck her knee into my side, knocking me over.

Annoyingly, I couldn't think of a single decent comeback or cutting remark. In fact, I hadn't managed to say anything at all, the whole time. I felt like a big fat dummy.

And that's exactly when you can fall back on your old friend, food.

So up I got and off I did trot to the glittering

lights of that palace of dreams, Burgerland. As
I was queuing up at the counter, I decided to
slightly modify my plan by getting a double
cheeseburger, fries and a Coke.

It was going to be a mighty big mouthful, but
I'd earned it.

I took my tray of goodness and found a table
in a sort of booth thing, which was nice and
secret, so nobody would see me doing my little
trick with Satan's toenail.

I managed to get one giant mouthful of
burger plus maybe seventeen fries in my mouth,
as well as a good swill of Coke.

Boy, it was good.

Little did I know that it was to be the high
point of the day. I fished the toenail out of my
pocket, black and curved and evil, and got ready
to put it in with the fries. But then I decided

that I'd have another bite – not a big whale-bite like the first one, but just a dainty little nibble. OK, it turned into another pretty big one. Let's say humpback whale rather than blue.

And then I had a thought. What had I done with the nail? I looked down at the tray with its cardboard cartons of food. I couldn't see it. I looked inside the burger bun, pulling it open to reveal the sticky cheese, gleaming like delicious orange snot.

And then I felt a tickle in my throat, and I knew what had become of the nail, and with that knowledge came the Bucking Steed of Panic. I suddenly started to feel most unwell. Sweat sprang out on my forehead. I didn't know if I should try to swallow what was in there, or spit it out. I imagined the sharp edge of the talon piercing the soft lining of my throat. But that was better than regurgitating my food, here in front of everyone . . .

I decided to try to swallow it down, thinking the mass of food would smooth the passage, and then my guts would do the rest.

Big mistake. Pain, sharp, terrifying. I stood up and bent over the plastic table. I opened my mouth and tried to empty out what was in there, letting a mass of chewed-up food just spill out, the way you'd empty the bin.

I was dimly aware that the door to the place had swung open, and that more people had come in. I vaguely sensed that I had become the centre of attention. But I didn't care, I truly didn't care: I could not breathe.

I was choking to death.

And if I didn't choke, the talon would soon work its way through the inside of my throat and

PIERCE MY JUGULAR VEIN!!!!!

I coughed, and coughed again, hoping to bring up the toenail. But it was no good. It was definitely stuck in my throat. My eyes were watering and I could hardly see anything, but I knew for sure that there was now a crowd around me.

Great.

I was going to die in Burgerland, in embarrassing agony, in front of loads of people.

Wearing my uncoolest elasticated trousers.

'Stand back. Let me through.'

The words were commanding and authoritative, and the voice was very familiar. I wiped my eyes with my sleeve and saw the bristling form of Mr Fricker approaching. Before I knew what was happening, he had positioned himself behind me, grabbed me under the arms,

and proceeded to punch me in the guts with his artificial hands, whilst jiggling me up and down in the time-honoured Heimlich manoeuvre.

Suddenly I felt the little monster in my throat budge. Fricker gave one final thrust, and with a sound like a bear breaking wind, the talon shot out of my mouth, whizzed across the room, pinged against a window, and then, with a kind of ghastly inevitability, got stuck in the hair of one of the girls who had just come in. One of

the girls I had just passed in the alleyway.

The hair, of course, belonged to Tamara Bello.

There was a second or two of silence before the uproar, which took the usual form of outraged squeals, appalled and disgusted yells, some fainting, and one sympathetic vomiting incident.

'GET IT OUT! GET IT OUT!' Tamara screamed, losing her cool for the first time ever since she got smacked on the bum by the midwife on the day she was born.

'I'm not touching it!' yelled one of the other girls. 'I don't even know what it is.'

'It looks like a bit of horse's hoof,' said another.

'You'll be fine now, boy,' said Mr Fricker, my handless saviour.

'Thanks,' I croaked.

'I always pay my debts,' said Fricker. 'But best

get on home. Whatever it was that was stuck in there may not have killed you, but this lot might.'

I took his advice and scuttled out of Burgerland, not even bothering to get my refund. I managed to slip in the vomit on the polished floor, but luckily didn't end up on my bum.

On the way home I scraped together enough change for a plain donut.

My plan now is to go to bed, pull the duvet over my head and eat the donut, hoping that its sweet and healing loveliness will obliterate the horrors of what was the worst day of my life.

DONUT COUNT:

Sunday 1 April

After the huge fiasco that was the whole of yesterday, today was a fairly quiet day, without any major traumas. You know how Sundays are always a bit rubbish, because the end of the weekend is nigh, and school looms up like a massive monstrous looming thing? Actually, that's usually a bit of an exaggeration, because normally the worst things that will happen to you on Monday are:

1. Several hours of intense boredom at the hands of geography, maths and French teachers;

2. Getting a break-time dead leg from a prefect;

3. Being forced to eat some kind of pinky-green meat paste stuff with a side order of vegetables that look like they've already been eaten and regurgitated at least once before, all served to you by a dinner lady with hatred in her eyes and some sort of brown matter under her fingernails that you hope against hope might just be congealed gravy, but which some deep part of your soul knows is the result of a fingers-bursting-through-the-toilet-paper situation;

4. Having to put up with a snide remark

from your enemy, the Floppy-Haired Kid, and possibly also a punch in the kidney from him when you're not looking.

Well, tomorrow I have none of those things to look forward to. Tomorrow it's going to be actual starvation combined with intense physical activity, plus having to sleep in a strange bed in a dormitory full of weird fat kids.

So today I hung out with my friend Jim, who doesn't go to our school. We played our spit-dribbling game, which involves dribbling spit (as you'd probably guessed) from the iron bridge over the canal. The point is to try to get a continuous strand of saliva to go all the way from your mouth to the water without breaking, and it's basically impossible if you haven't got a cold.

Unfortunately
a duck chose that
moment to swim
under the bridge, and
got some spit on its
back. We aren't the
kind of kids who like
spitting on ducks, so
we decided to stop
the game.

Then I told Jim
about my food
fiasco of the day
before, which made
him laugh so hard I
thought he was going
to fall in the canal.

I thought about being annoyed, but then I realized that it was actually quite funny, and I suddenly felt a bit better, laughter being the great healer and all that.

And then Jim slightly ruined things by saying, 'You do, don't you?'

And I, like an idiot, said, 'I do what, don't I?'

'Fancy her!'

I didn't even dignify the question with an answer, but stomped off home.

There was supposed to be a nice last meal with my family before I left for Camp Fatso, not that the word 'nice' is normally associated with the Milligans.

It didn't happen, of course.

Before it even got going, my mum and dad had a big row about the whole sending-me-away thing. My dad said he didn't approve of 'fascist health prison camps', and my mum said that it was his fault that I was overweight, although it really isn't. It's my fault. And the fault of donuts for being so delicious.

Because they were arguing, the low-fat vegetable lasagne got so burned it looked like a blackened cowpat, and we had to have cottage cheese on crackers instead.

I kind of expected Ruby and Ella to be nasty to me in their own different ways, with Ruby talking to me in her evil baby voice, going, 'Ooooh, the poor fat Dodo has to go to a nasty prison for fatties, and he won't get any of his naughty donuts, will he, poor ickle-wickle baby,' etc., etc., and Ella giving me one of her scary silent stares, while sticking needles into a fat voodoo doll under the table and maybe draining my blood to be used in some ceremony involving toads.

In fact, they were OK. I don't mean they were actually pleasant or anything, but they didn't attack me physically or verbally. Perhaps they are human after all, and not just androids sent back through time to destroy my life.

Actually, Ruby and Ella acting all decent made me even more depressed than a full-frontal assault would have done. It somehow hammered home the grimness of what I faced.

Luckily, before I went upstairs, Ruby said, 'Listen, Dermot, if you take any of my stuff to fat camp, I'm going to scrape the skin off my verruca into your bed so when you get home you get covered in verrucas all over your body.'

I thought about saying that there was nothing that she owned that I wouldn't happily have burned in a giant bonfire, even if the resulting pink cloud would block out the sun and bring on a new ice age causing the destruction of civilization as we know it. But I didn't have the fight in me.

'Sure,' I said, and shrugged.

DONUT COUNT:

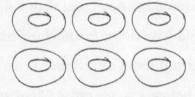

Last day, so had to fortify myself for what was to come.

Monday 2 April

1 p.m.

It was supposed to be a two-hour drive to Camp Fatso. The plan was to set off at 7 a.m. to get there for the 9 a.m. start. My mum was taking me because my dad's lost his licence. I don't mean that the police took it away from him or anything, just that he put it down somewhere and now can't find it.

Things went wrong from the beginning. First

my alarm clock didn't quack (it's shaped like a duck and I've been meaning to destroy it for years now) and then the car wouldn't start, so we had to call the AA man, who turned out to be the AA lady, and it took her half an hour to sort out the problem. And then we got really badly lost because I was in charge of directions and I got confused about the difference between Sussex and Suffolk when I put the address into the sat-nav.

It all meant that we were hours and hours late.

When our sat-nav told us that we were about five miles from Camp Fatso, we drove through a small village with nothing much in it except a pub called the Slaughtered Lamb and a closed-down petrol station and a shop that sold doormats.

After the village, the road twisted and turned

like a snake having a fight with another snake, and it took a further fifteen minutes to get to Camp Fatso. The countryside gradually changed from fields with cows in (one of which was having a giant green wee) to woodland. It should have been pretty in a countrysidey sort of way. But the trees were too close together for my liking, so it all seemed sort of gloomy and depressing and a little bit threatening.

'This is lovely,' said Mum. 'It's a bit like a fairy-tale forest.'

Did I really need to explain to her what happens in fairy tales? That kids get abandoned by their evil parents? That they get eaten by wolves? Imprisoned and tortured by witches? Forced to do silly dances while wearing those shoes with curly-wurly toes?

I didn't ever want to have to wear those shoes.

But I knew that she was only saying it because she needed to believe that she was taking me somewhere nice.*

My first sighting of Camp Fatso was a tall wooden tower that loomed over the trees. A flag was flying from the top of the tower. The flag had a picture of a rosy-cheeked kid, grinning like an idiot who'd finally got a joke two days after he'd heard it. Then there was a sign at the side of the road saying CAMP FATSO, and we turned off. We bumped along a track for a few more minutes until we came to a wooden gateway. Above the gateway there was a banner that read:

* Throughout history, many of the greatest atrocities have been committed by people who thought they were doing something good, like the Spanish Inquisition and the man who invented cauliflower cheese.

CAMP FATSO: GET FIT HAVING FUN!

There was a man at the gate wearing a black
tracksuit and carrying a clipboard. There was
something weird on his head, like a sort of
Cornish pasty made of hair. I'd say it was a wig,

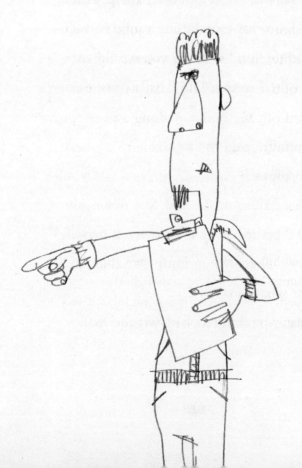

except that no one, surely, would knowingly wear a wig that looked so much like a wig? It might as well have had a giant arrow above it, inscribed with the words THIS IS A WIG.

He looked at his watch and said, 'Just arrived?'

I wanted very much to say, 'Duh!' but I didn't. We've all decided at school that saying, 'Duh!' when someone says something stupid is itself stupid, and the kind of thing you would say, 'Duh!' about, if saying, 'Duh!' hadn't just been banned.

'Sorry, traffic,' said my mum.

'Name, please.'

'Dermot Milligan,' she said. She obviously thought I'd get it wrong if I answered myself, and I'd say Dilbert Minigun or Dr Sebastian Banana or whatever.

The black-tracksuited, bad-wigged man

66

looked at his clipboard.

'Ah, yes. Excellent. Out you get, young man.'

'Can't I drive him in?' asked my mum, looking a bit worried.

'Sorry, 'fraid not. No cars. And you'll have to say your goodbyes here. We've found it just makes things more difficult for the young people if their parents or carers hang around. I'll take Dermot up to reception.'

I grabbed my bag from the boot and tried to escape before my mum could give me a hug, but she was too clever for me.

'You'll need some money,' she said, holding out a twenty-pound note. I had to climb back into the car to get it, and that meant a hug, two kisses and a splashing of tears.

'I'm really proud of you for this,' she said. 'It takes guts to do what you're doing.'

I had a quick look around. No one was there to see, except Badwig, and I guessed he'd seen it all before.

'Yeah, well,' I said, patting my ample stomach, 'got plenty of those.'

Another squeeze, and then I escaped. I trudged through the gates carrying my bag, which was so heavy I wondered for a moment if my mum hadn't somehow managed to sneak herself into it.

'Right, Milligan,' said Badwig as soon as my mum was out of sight. 'You're in for a wonderful time. But let's get off on the right foot, shall we? So stand up straight, and quick march.'

'March?'

'That's right. Swing your arms, one–two, one–two.'

This was not a good start. I mean –
marching . . . ?

And my first sighting of the inside of Camp
Fatso wasn't very promising either.

I could see a number of long wooden huts
and various other buildings. The tower I had
seen from the road was one of four, each placed
at a corner of a high perimeter fence. I couldn't
see any machine guns up there, but that didn't
mean there weren't any. Back on ground level,
there was a sports field, marked with various
mysterious white lines. Clusters of overweight
kids were doing various equally mysterious
things around the field, overseen by more adults
in black. The kids were wearing bright orange
tracksuits.

Orange is not a good colour for fat people.
Take a kid who is more or less round, and dress

him (or her, if it's a female fatty) in orange, and what you have, basically, is an orange. A similar effect can be had by taking tall, slightly curved kids and dressing them in yellow.

Badwig marched me into one of the buildings. There were a couple of muscle-bound adults in there, lounging around and drinking those protein shakes that bodybuilders slurp all day. They looked me up and down and then one whispered to the other, and they both burst out laughing. In my experience, anything that begins with being laughed at doesn't usually end very well.

'This is Milligan,' said Badwig, and the final tiny bit of friendliness had gone out of his voice. Then he added, ominously, 'The last of them . . .'

Then he opened up a counter and moved behind it. This involved stepping over something on the floor. For a second I thought it was a large stain; then I saw that it was alive, and I briefly contemplated the possibility that it might be a new species of giant weasel. Then I realized that it wasn't a large or giant version of a small thing, but a small version of a big thing. A dog. A sausage dog, to be precise.

I've never liked sausage dogs. They look sly and evil to me, but the main thing is that they take themselves sooooo seriously, and don't realize how fundamentally silly they are. Taking yourself seriously is perfectly OK if you're the Prime Minister or a professor of philosophy, but there's absolutely no excuse for it if you're a dog and you look like a sausage.

And I know that the real name for a sausage dog is a datchhund, dachunte, doushhound or dachshund, but I can never remember how to spell it, so I prefer to stick with sausage dog.

Oh yes, and the other thing about sausage dogs is that they really hate me. I can't say which came first, the me-hating-them or the them-hating-me. It's a chicken-and-egg situation. But all you have to remember is that me and sausage dogs don't get on.

But I thought I could at least make an effort, so I tried to stroke the dog. He snapped at me as if he'd been waiting all day for the chance to eat some poor fat kid's fingers.

'Meet Gustav,' said Badwig. 'He's Boss Skinner's dog, so you'd best watch him.'

'Boss Skinner . . . who's he?'

Badwig and the others laughed.

'Oh, you'll find out soon enough. Right, put your bag up here.'

'My bag? Er, OK.'

Not really knowing what to expect, I heaved the bag up onto the counter. Then, to my amazement, Badwig unzipped it, and had a good old root through it, like we were in airport security.

'You can't do that,' I said. 'It's private!'

I heard more harsh laughter from behind me.

'Got something to hide, have you, Milligan?' said Badwig.

'No, but I . . .'

'And what have we here?' he continued.

I knew what we had here.

'Is it a treat for Gustav? Oh yes, I think it is.'

He held up a paper bag with four donuts in it.

'Naughty, naughty,' he said, and I felt myself blushing.

'They were just . . .' Just what? They were just donuts, and they weren't allowed.

'Well, you won't be needing those in Camp Fatso,' said Badwig.

Then, right before my eyes, he started feeding my donuts to the horrible dog. I honestly wouldn't have minded sacrificing my donuts to help starving children in Africa, or even to feed quite hungry donkeys abandoned by their owners in, er, wherever donkeys live. But giving them to a SAUSAGE DOG! It was sacrilege.

'And you can't take these into Camp Fatso either,' he said, taking my laptop and phone out of my bag.

I'd anticipated this, and I had an argument ready.

'My nutritionist says I have to keep a daily diary of what I eat, so—'

'Tough. There are no sockets in the dorms or anywhere else to charge electronic devices, so it won't be of any use to you.'

That was seriously bad news. The laptop was loaded up with games and movies.

Badwig put a neatly folded set of orange clothing on the counter.

'Get changed into these,' he ordered.

'Er, where?'

'Just in the corner over there.'

Now, I don't know about you, but one of my

pet hates is taking off my clothes in public, so I didn't exactly leap to it.

'Get on with it,' said Badwig. 'Don't worry, we're not looking, are we, Gustav?'

Gustav didn't reply – he was too busy eating my donuts.

And so I did. Stupid, I know. I should have told them to get stuffed and called my mum, and got the heck out of there, but somehow I'd been institutionalized already, and found it impossible not to obey orders.

And of course, halfway through getting changed I found myself under attack by the sausage dog of doom, who'd finished my donuts and decided on a bit of sport to work off the calories. He yapped and nipped at my ankles while I flapped at him with my trousers.

Finally Badwig came round the counter

and picked up Gustav.

'That's a good boy,' he said.

By that stage I'd managed to change into the shiny orange tracksuit. You can imagine how ridiculous I looked. If you can't imagine, then I'll tell you: I looked *extremely* ridiculous.

'Right,' said Badwig. 'Now you're kitted out, you can get along to your hut. It's number four. Turn left outside. You've missed lunch and you're too late for afternoon PE, so just hang around until the others come in.'

I went to grab my bag.

'Oh no,' said Badwig. 'This goes in the store room with all the others.'

'But my things . . . my toothbrush . . .'

Badwig pulled out my wash bag. 'You can take this. Off you go now. The latrines and showers are in the blue building on the way.'

So, giving my bag a last lingering look, I left the office. Gustav had another snap at me, and I hurried down the steps to get out of range, already planning an elaborate revenge.

The hut was easy to find. I walked slowly along the gravel path, passing Huts One, Two and Three. They were brightly painted in rainbow colours, but that couldn't hide the fact that they were pretty run-down and shabby.

I reached Hut Four and walked up the wooden steps. Inside there were six bunk beds, a rough table and an iron stove. It was both cold and stuffy. There was a strong and unpleasant odour of boy: that mix of methane, armpit-juice and foot-cheese. Of course there was no telly, so that's when I decided to write up the first part of the day.

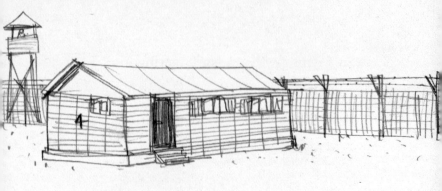

But of course I had nothing to write on.
By then I needed a wee so I found the latrine
hut. It was draughty and cold and miserable,
and the toilet paper was that painfully hard and
unabsorbent stuff they used to have in World
War Two.

But at least I'd found something to write
on. Now I'm wondering if this is the first ever
journal written on toilet paper?

I await the arrival of my hut mates . . .

Monday 2 April

8 p.m.

You know those books and movies where the hero goes to sleep and wakes up in an alternative reality that turns out to be a demon dimension, or maybe even hell itself? Well, I think I might be in one of those.

I didn't have to wait long in the hut before the others began to turn up. I was expecting it to be mainly fatties. However, it really was a parade of all shapes and sizes that came trudging through the door into the hut.

The first to come in was a black kid, who looked pretty tough. Or at least as tough as you can look when you're wearing dirty orange pyjamas.

Next came a conventional fatty, like me, but drawn by a cartoonist so that everything was even rounder. His face was lost in flab, so it looked like someone had thrown a lump of dough at his head, where it had stuck. He glanced nervously at me, and then down at the ground, mumbling something to himself, as the others stomped in behind him.

The next was a giant kid – not so much fat as generally huge. His head clanged on the iron lightshade dangling from the ceiling. He had hands like the bucket scoop on a digger.

Irregular clumps of hair were arranged randomly
over his scalp, separated by areas of scabby,
stubbly skin. It was not a good advert for cutting
your own hair with a set of blunt gardening
shears. All in all, he looked very much like
an ogre, which made me think again of what
my mum had said about the place being like
something from a fairy tale.

Next came a weedy, grey-faced specimen, with constellations of boils and spots sprayed over his face. Yep, I could make out the Great Bear, Orion's Belt and the Big Dipper, all done in zit-form. He wasn't fat at all, just vaguely unhealthy-looking, as if he'd spent his entire life locked in the school toilet. He had the sort of furtive, slightly ratty look to him that's gone completely out of fashion. Except among rats.

After him, a big fat Chinese kid waddled in, looking like a juvenile sumo wrestler. I wondered if he was a black belt in some kind of ninja stuff, like throwing those little death-star thingies or whacking people with two sticks joined by a chain. Then I realized that it was probably racist to assume that anyone of Chinese or Japanese descent is good at throwing ninja death stars, so I decided to stop thinking like that, and just assume that he was a simple fatty, like the rest of us.

'Hi,' I said, as they all gathered around me. I thought they were being friendly until I noticed their faces. They each stared blankly at me, as if I'd already managed to do something to make them hate me.

'So who crapped in your lunch boxes?' I said, trying to win them over with a bit of feisty humour.

I may as well have been trying to win over a man-eating tiger by offering it a banana.

'Newbie,' said the tough-looking black kid in an American accent.

The ogre made a sort of rumbling noise. It sounded like he was saying, 'Doom.'

'And what do we do to newbies?' continued the black kid.

The others all yelled in unison, 'PILE ON!'

And that's what they did.

It was like being jumped on by a family of mammoths.

Now, you've probably had a pile on at school, when you all basically pile on top of everyone else (hence the name). It's quite a good laugh, and the kid at the bottom hardly ever has to go to hospital or suffers long-term brain damage.

But this was different. This was an Olympic-level pile on. I had the weight of four titanic fatties and one spotty kid pressing down on me. My calculations show that this is equivalent, in terms of pressure per square inch, to the conditions on the surface of Venus and at the bottom of the ocean, i.e. totally blinking FATAL.

I tried to scream for help but there was zero air in my lungs. I thought I was going to die.

Squashed flat by kids even fatter than me. What a way to go. And I hadn't even had lunch.

And that's when I remembered it. The wash bag. It was on the floor, just a few centimetres away, a picture of Homer Simpson smiling on the front of it.

Luckily, although I was pinned under the living mound of flesh, I could move my right arm just enough to reach the wash bag. I managed to slip my fingers into it, and found what I was looking for.

The wash-bag donut! I thought that it would save me from hunger, but now it was going to save me from death.

I knew that any kids who'd been here for a while would be craving sweet things the way a vampire craves the slender neck of a young girl. With a flick of my wrist I sent the donut (chocolate icing, hundreds and thousands, a bit squashed) skittering across the wooden floor of the hut.

I don't know who saw (or smelled) it first, but I heard the cry of 'Donut!' go up, and suddenly I was free. I looked over to see a writhing mass of fat humanity fighting over the sugary treat. They were like sharks on a feeding frenzy; like vultures tucking into an opened-up wildebeest belly; like grannies at a jumble sale.

Only the black American kid wasn't partaking in the scramble. He stood off to one side, shaking his head slowly, as if disappointed by the performance.

Finally, the spotty kid used his superior speed and got hold of the donut. He was about to chomp on it when, from either side, the ogre and the dough-faced boy dived in, their mouths open, like blue whales eating krill. Their huge jaws bit off the two 'wings' of the donut, leaving just the middle section. The spotty kid tried desperately to lift it up to his mouth, but it never got there. The Chinese boy now grabbed the spotty kid's hand. They wrestled for a few seconds, and then the Chinese boy opened his huge mouth and engulfed the hand that still clung to the remains of the donut. I thought he was going to chew that hand right off, but it seemed he just sucked the donut pulp out of it, for when the spotty kid finally pulled his hand back out, it was as clean as a whistle, but also slightly puckered and wrinkled, like when you've been in the bath too long.

All the way through, the black kid stood aloof in one corner, his eyes half closed.

'Got any more?' asked the pimply kid.

I shrugged. 'Maybe. For my friends.'

They looked at each other. Then the black kid stepped towards me.

'We can be friends. In fact, your hut buddies are the only friends you'll ever have in this joint.'

'Yeah,' said the spotty one, 'we stick by each other. Without us, you is nothing.'

'You've got a funny way of showing it,' I said, dusting myself down.

'You're the new kid. What did you expect?' said Spotty.

I shrugged. 'Not getting squashed to death, maybe . . . ?'

'You're breathing, ain't you?' said the black

kid. 'So where are the cakes, huh?'

'They're in a secret compartment in—'

'In your bag,' he said, finishing my sentence. The other kids all joined in with a collective groan. 'Well, you can say goodbye to those suckers. You figure you're the only kid who ever tried sneaking food in here like that? You'll never see those donuts again.'

'But they can't—'

'They can do anything they want to.'

At that moment, the door was thrown open and two of the black-clad guards came in. One was my old friend Badwig, which didn't exactly fill my soul with joy, but the other looked much scarier. He was as lean as a whippet, and had slate-grey hair and slate-grey features, and a jaw so square it made other squares look like badly drawn circles. I thought I was seeing things for a second – there seemed to be a machine gun on a strap across his shoulders. They weren't allowed to carry arms, were they? Then I realized that it was a paintball gun – Jim had had a paintballing birthday party last year. It would have been fun if it wasn't for the fact that I attracted most of the enemy fire, being the biggest target. And let me tell you, those paintballs really, really hurt when they hit you.

A snarl from ground level alerted me to the third member of the party: Gustav, the evil sausage dog.

'Fall in line!' yelled Badwig.

Instantly the other inmates of Hut Four did just that, forming a neat, if rather fat, line, like currant buns in a packet. I joined them.

Badwig stood to one side while the scary guard walked silently along the line, staring each of the kids in the eye. Gustav followed him, growling and snapping at shins and ankles.

Then, just before he got to me, the lean, mean, grey guard glanced down at his feet. His face changed. He looked puzzled for a moment. Then he lifted up his foot and examined the sole. He put his finger to it and then raised the finger to his mouth. A thin, lizard-like tongue shot out.

I realized what it was he'd seen: donut crumbs!

The scary guard spoke in a voice that was barely more than a whisper.

'What is the meaning of this?'

It wasn't clear who he was speaking to, so no one answered.

The silence in the hut weighed about a million tons.

'I will count to three. If I do not have an

answer by then, this hut will be subjected to collective punishment.'

He didn't specify what the collective punishment was, but I guessed it was unlikely to be losing the chance of a second scoop of ice cream at dinner time.

Then I had a little brainwave. Or a mild attack of insanity.

'It was me,' I said. Then I added a 'sir'. Not sure why, it just seemed wise.

You're probably wondering why I did this. The owning-up bit, I mean.

Well, my thinking was as follows:

1. It was going to make me look good in front of my new hut mates.
2. As we were going to be stuck together for the next two weeks, it was important

that we get on.

3. It would make them less likely to squash me to death.

4. I didn't think the punishment was likely to be that bad.

5. It *was*, actually, my donut, even if I hadn't eaten it.

The chiselled jaw swivelled my way, like a machine-gun turret on a German bomber. The owner of the jaw had pale-blue eyes, strongly suggesting the capacity for Infinite Cruelty.*

---

* Actually, I don't suppose eye colour really has anything to do with how cruel you are. There may well be people with pale-blue eyes who are incredibly kind and who constantly rescue cats out of trees and give all their sweets to the poor. And I'm sure there are other people with kindly brown eyes who make a living by torturing monkeys and forcing dogs to smoke cigarettes. But you know what I mean.

A hissing sound emerged from the thin-lipped mouth. Suddenly he was right in front of me. There was a faint smell of decay, thinly masked with mouthwash. He was shorter than I'd expected – we were about the same height.

'Do I look like I've been knighted?' he said, his voice still as quiet as a butterfly landing on a dandelion.

Badwig took a step towards the other guard and said, 'He's new, Boss Skinner . . .'

I don't know if he was actually trying to help me out, or just sucking up to skinny Skinner.

Skinner said not a word back, but merely thrust out his hand. I thought for a second he was going to smack Badwig, but he was just silencing him. The other guard stepped back again, looking like a scolded puppy.

'I asked you a question.'

'N–no, sir.'

I don't know what it was about being called 'sir' that upset the little maniac, but now he burned with a cold, silent rage that made him speak, if anything, even more quietly.

'My name is Boss Skinner. You call me Boss Skinner or plain Boss and nothing else. Understand that?'

'Er, yes. I mean, yes, Boss Skinner.'

'Do I need to get my hound here to help you remember?' He exchanged significant looks with Gustav, who stood alert and ready to strike. He definitely had the look of a sausage dog that wanted to eat some ankles.

'No, Boss.'

Now the whisper was back, like a breeze through a forest of razor blades.

'You brought food in here.'

'I-I-I—'

'You brought bad food in here. Forbidden food.'

'Boss Skinner, I didn't—'

The hand came up again. It was impossible to carry on.

Boss Skinner took off his trainer.

He looked at the sole. He held it up to me. There were mashed donut crumbs squeezed up into the tread. He brushed the crumbs onto the floor. Gustav moved greedily towards them, but froze as his master whispered, 'No!'

'You lick it up,' he said to me.

'What, Boss Skinner?'

I glanced along the line. Most of the other kids were staring straight ahead. But the Chinese kid was looking at me. His eyes were wide open and he shook his head, as if in warning.

'I said lick it up. Unless you want to spend a week in the cooler.'

Whatever the cooler was, I didn't want to go there. And more than that, there was something about Boss Skinner that made it impossible to stand up to him. So I got down on my hands and knees. I was actually about to lick the crumbs off the floor, despite the envious growling of Gustav, when I realized that something was happening. There was movement all around. I looked up. The other kids had all got down on their hands and knees, too. They looked like a herd of cows.

I glanced quickly at Boss Skinner. His face had turned even greyer than before, and his lips had completely disappeared. If you were going to enter a competition to paint the Most Evil Face Imaginable by the Human Brain, and you handed in a picture of Boss Skinner looking like he did right now, you'd definitely win. Or at least come third, assuming the top two spots had gone to Adolf Hitler and Lord Voldemort.

I think at that point one of the kids actually mooed. You know, like a cow. And then someone else did, and soon the whole herd of fatties was mooing. Plus giggling, which slightly spoiled the cow-effect, the bovine race not being known as big gigglers.

Gustav didn't like the mooing, and he backed off, whining. Maybe he'd had a bad experience with a cow.

Anyway, the upshot was that Boss Skinner's attempt to destroy me on my first day had turned to farce. He ground his teeth, and then spun round and marched out of there, with Badwig and Gustav on his heels.

I got up, and most of the others got up as well, although the dough-faced boy stayed on to finish up the crumbs.

'Thanks,' I said to the black kid. 'That was decent of you. I mean, doing that cow thing.'

He nodded, his face still impassive. 'Like I

said, hut buddies gotta stick together. 'Specially against Boss Skinner. That man's a psychopath, even by the standards of this place. Anyway, you owned up for the donut, and that gets you some respect around here. What's your name, kid?'

I thought for a moment. Dermot or Donut? I was called both at school.

'Call me Donut,' I said.

He chuckled and put out a chunky hand. 'I'm Jermaine. They call me J-Man. Meet the gang.'

He gestured to the Chinese kid.

'This is Dong. His parents sent him over here from Beijing, and he don't speak a whole lot of English.'

Dong gave a little bow.

'Hello, old chap, delighted to make your acquaintance,' he said in perfect English.

I look quizzically at J-Man.

'Yeah, he starts off well, but that's it: you now heard the sum total of his conversation.'

'Hello, old chap, delighted to make your acquaintance,' Dong said again, as if to confirm this.

The dough-faced boy came forward. 'This is Florian Frost,' J-Man said. 'We all call him Flo.'

'Nice to meet you,' said Flo very quickly, in a high-pitched squeaky voice. He was looking at the floor again. 'I like bugs, but not to eat. I sometimes lick them, just to taste, but I wouldn't hurt one. Bugs like to be licked. Did you know that we've discovered four hundred thousand species of beetle, but there could be as many as twelve million, yes, I said twelve million, and at the current rate of discovery we won't have named them all until the sun expands and obliterates us, which makes me sad, very sad, yes, it does, thinking of all those beetles without names.'

The kid was clearly distressed by this, and J-Man comforted him.

'It's OK, Flo, it's OK,' he said, putting his arm around Flo's shoulders. 'You'll name them beetles, I know you will. Let's get your softy.'

J-Man took Flo over to his bunk and gave him his softy, which turned out to be a cuddly toy beetle, the size of a teddy bear.

'Flo's a genius-level brainiac,' said J-Man when he came back. 'But he's not too good with people.'

Then the huge ogre shambled over.

'This is Igor,' said J-Man. 'His real name's Quentin, but he just doesn't suit that. But don't let appearances deceive you. He's a sweet kid. Just don't get between him and his gruel or he'll put his hand down your throat all the way to your knees and turn you inside out. And believe me, nobody wants to see your guts on the outside of you.'

Igor and I exchanged nods. I quickly made up a little poem to help me remember Igor and his foibles:

Only a fool
Would mess with Igor's gruel;
So don't, or you'll
Be in for a shock
When he turns you inside out like a sock.

Not my greatest ever poem, I admit, but I made it up on the spot in my head, so you have to make allowances.

Last, I met the spotty kid, who was called Ernesto Gogol. Ernesto creeped me out a bit: his front teeth seemed to have been filed to points. Either that or they were just naturally pointy, but as far as I'm aware, pointed front teeth just aren't part of the human genome, belonging more properly to the world of bats, cats and rats.

Suddenly a siren whined, wailed and screamed. It sounded like a vat of bats, cats and rats being baked alive.

'What the heck's that?' I said. 'An air raid?'

But I got no reply from J-Man, for the droning of that siren had a bizarre and deeply unsettling effect on the inmates of Hut Four. J-Man stopped literally halfway through a word. His eyes glazed over, and I thought I saw the glistening of a little line of drool at the corner of his mouth. He didn't quite put his hands straight out and start groaning, zombie style, but it wasn't a million miles away from that. He was not alone. The others all looked the same.*

J-Man turned away from me and, along with the others, headed out the door. Outside, I saw lines of fat zombies streaming from all the other huts in the compound. The lines converged, and together they trudged towards the mess hall. It was like one of those massive migrations you see on nature programmes, you know – wildebeest on the Serengeti.

I didn't know what else to do, so I followed along. I found myself behind the giant, Igor. I tapped him on the shoulder, meaning to ask him what was going on, but he just shrugged me off, making one of his grunts.

---

* If, on the zombie scale, one represents Albert Einstein and ten represents a full-blown, brain-eating member of the undead, then J-Man and the rest of Hut Four were suddenly scoring a highly creditable seven.

From the outside, the mess hut simply looked like a bigger version of the dormitory huts. However, its smell was even worse. There's some kind of cosmic law that says that wherever kids are compelled to eat, there must be the accompanying smell of cabbage. I reckon that even in school dining halls for Eskimos in Greenland, where there isn't an actual cabbage for, like, ten thousand miles, and all they eat are dolphins and snow, there's still a good old cabbagey smell, like a donkey farted into a bag of brussels sprouts.

I followed Igor in, and found a typical canteen, with a counter at one end and tables crowded together, in no recognizable order. Except there *was* a sort of order – each table had a little red flag with a number on it. One for each hut, I guessed.

I say it was a typical canteen, but there was

a major difference: I'd never seen so many humungously fat kids gathered together. For the first time in my life I was, well, ordinary.

In some ways it was kind of liberating, not to stand out. Usually I wasn't Dermot Milligan, human being, but Donut, fat kid. People looked at me and saw, not someone with a brain and ideas and feelings and all the usual things that kids have, but a big wobbly gut on legs.

But on another level I sort of missed it. Now I was just part of this huge herd of fatties. At least out there, in the real world, I stood out.

I joined the queue at the food counter. Close up, the smell was even worse. I could feel it seeping into my clothes and hair. It was going to take a long time to wash the cabbagey stench off. In fact, I might never wash it off. I imagined being at university and still smelling of cabbage.

Getting married. Working in an office. A whole life of people edging away from me because they thought I'd let fly with a silent guff. Or worse, because they thought I just smelled like that naturally. It would only be in old age that I'd find peace and acceptance, because all old people smell of cabbage, so I'd fit right in.

As we all shuffled forward, a sudden wave of excitement went through the line. I heard a sound. It gradually formed itself into a recognizable word.

'Meat.'

That was a nice surprise. In the DVD about the place they'd only ever mentioned the fresh fruit and vegetables . . .

Anyway, I finally reached the front of the queue. By this stage I was starving, as I'd had nothing to eat since breakfast, and it was dinner time now.

The dinner ladies were reassuringly normal. For dinner ladies, I mean. Compared to most normal humans they were pretty gross. There were three of them. One ladled gruel into bowls, another dolloped a slice of some kind of dark meat on top of the gruel and a third supervised in case the ladling and dolloping was being performed in some irregular manner.

I received my gruel. It was grey and thin, like the last bit of puke that comes out when you've got nothing left to heave up. And, like all true vomit the world over, it had little bits of carrot in it.

The second dinner lady was about to chuck the dark meat on my plate.

'Can I ask what it is?' I said.

She looked at me through her thick glasses

for a while. Her name badge said URSULA, but she didn't look much like an Ursula. She looked more like a THLUGG. Or possibly a NORA. She finally replied in a monotone, 'Nutritionally rounded food product.'

I stared more closely at the meat. Like I said, it was mainly a dark brown colour, but now I could see that there was a marbling of grey, and some unsettling pink highlights. It looked like a failed attempt to create life in a horror film.

'Animal, mineral or vegetable?' I asked, trying to make a joke with the one called Ursula. There was a long pause, and I sensed the queue of fatties getting agitated behind me. Ursula's mouth moved but nothing intelligible came out. Finally the supervisor stepped in.

'It's absolutely guaranteed fresh,' she said sharply, as if that answered everything.

My plate loaded up with gruel and nutritionally rounded food product, I went to sit with the others at the Hut Four table. The rest of them were already munching, and as they ate I sensed that they were gradually getting back to normal. The zombie thing must just have been low blood sugar.

'Do you reckon I could kill this thing with salt, the way you do with slugs?' I said, pointing at the meat with my fork. I meant it as a joke, but nobody laughed.

'Don't you want it?' asked J-Man. There was a hungry light in his eyes. I looked back at the brown slab. I truly didn't want it.

'Nope.'

Moving so quickly the eye could hardly follow it, J-Man speared the meat, cut it up, and distributed it to the rest of the table. They devoured their portions like rabid werewolves.

I ate the gruel.

It tasted cruel.*

I checked out the other tables. To begin
with they all appeared more or less the same
– filled with identikit plump kids. But now I
thought I could see some differences. One table,
in particular, stood out. The kids there were
enormous, but they weren't just big: they looked
kind of mean. As if to confirm my thought, I saw
a leg shoot out from the table to trip up a kid
waddling by. He stumbled and his gruel spilled

---

* Thought I might try another poem, but I've run
  out of rhymes. That can happen to even the greatest
  wordsmiths. There's a famous poem called *Paradise Lost*
  by John Milton, and it's about five hundred pages long,
  and Milton couldn't even think of a single rhyme in
  the whole poem – I know, because I had a quick check.
  And despite that, Milton is totally famous. Weird.

on the floor. I moved to help him. But J-Man put his hand on my arm.

'Careful, Donut,' he said in a quiet voice. 'That's the Lardies. You don't mess with them, or they will mess you up. And when the Lardies mess you up, you stayed messed.'

'The Lardies? Who are they? *What* are they?'

'The Lardies help run this place the way the goons like it run.'

'Goons?'

'Yeah, you know, the guards in the black uniforms. We call them the goons. Anyway, they don't like to bother with any of the actual brutalization, unless they have to. So they send the Lardies in to sit on any kids who fall out of line.'

'But what's in it for them? I mean, why do the Lardies do it?'

'Back in their huts those boys got all the good things we don't get no sight of. Candy, potato chips, soda pop, whatever they want. And it's not just the food,' continued J-Man. 'Those guys control everything else in here. The gambling, the bun running—'

'The what?'

'Bun running. They smuggle extra food into the camp and sell it to anyone who's got the money.'

'But they took our money when we arrived.'

'Some guys are cleverer than you at hiding it. Others get it passed in through the fence. Some steal it.'

Before J-Man had the chance to tell me anything else about the set-up of the camp, an amplified voice rang out from the other end of the mess hall.

'Testing, testing, one-two-three.'

It was Badwig, his Cornish-pasty hairdo newly polished, testing the mic.

And there, standing behind Badwig, was Boss Skinner. He moved his head from side to side, eyeballing the crowd, and looking for all the world like a Terminator sent back through time to destroy fat kids. The faithful Gustav was by his side, doing his doggy version of the Skinner stare.

J-Man leaned closer. 'Just because the guy with the hair does the talkin', don't you be thinkin' he's got the power. The power is—'

'Skinner, I know.'

'There's bigger bosses than Boss Skinner,' said J-Man mysteriously.

'Inmates of Camp Fatso,' Badwig continued in his whiny voice. 'It is my pleasure to welcome those who joined us today for the first time. I trust that our longer-term residents will make them suitably welcome.'

This was followed by a sort of growl from the mob, indicating that the sort of welcome they had in mind for us was that given to the Christians by the lions in the Roman arena.

'There are a couple of announcements I have to make. Tomorrow morning's run will now begin at six a.m. rather than at six thirty.' This was met with a groan of dismay.

'SILENCE!' hissed Boss Skinner. His whisper penetrated further than the amplified whine of Badwig. Normally groaning isn't something you can help doing, but nobody groaned after that.

'And in order to maximize the amount of time you are able to spend in healthy outdoor activities, from now on you will each be given a packed lunch.'

There were some muffled cheers at this. I guessed it was because people thought it would be an improvement on the gruel.

'Finally, a warning. There was an attempt by one of the new boys to smuggle food into the camp. THIS WILL NOT BE TOLERATED. Any further incidents of this kind will be dealt with severely. The solitary meditation chambers await anyone caught infringing our food regulations.'

I looked over at J-Man and shrugged.

'The cooler,' he mouthed back.

After dinner we trudged back to Hut Four. It was dark and cold and dismal outside, and dark and cold and dismal inside, as well, especially once the lights went off at 9 p.m. Yep, you read that right. 9 p.m. That's not been my bed time since Year Three.

After that, the only illumination was an eerie

blue glow as Dong and Ernesto took it in turns to light each other's farts. Which was funny for the first seventeen times . . .

And no one has ever managed to read or write by the light of ignited bum-blasts, but luckily I found the stub of an old candle. There were funny little indentations in it, which puzzled me until I realized that they were tooth marks: yep, some poor kid had tried to eat it, to counteract the terrible hunger pangs we've all got.

And so ends the weirdest day of my life, and

undoubtedly one of the most depressing. And
I've got a feeling it's all going to get worse.

DONUT COUNT:

I got a few of the crumbs from the wash-bag
donut.

Tuesday 3 April

There is always a certain satisfaction in being right, even if it means that HORROR WILL BE HEAPED ON HORROR IN A NEVERENDING CASCADE OF ROTTENNESS.

The day began (or rather, the night ended) with me in the middle of a dream that was both brilliant and terrible at the same time. I was in a flying donut, equipped for space travel, and I was cruising along somewhere in the region of Uranus.* Of course, I had to zap a few bug-eyed aliens, including Admiral Thlugg and the Borgia Empire, which was kind of fun. But then I got peckish and started eating my own spacecraft, which is totally against Star Command regulations, but, you know, I was hungry. So I had this terrible anxiety eating away at me just as I was eating away at my ship. It was a classic rock-and-hard-place scenario: I had the terrible choice of eating my donut ship and dying a horrible space death or NOT EATING A GIANT DONUT!!!!!

I was saved from the horns of this dilemma by the sound of my neutrino engines over-heating (which was the result, I guess, of my over-eating,

---

* I know you want to, but don't say it – the word 'Uranus' hasn't actually been funny for years. Well, OK, it is still quite funny, but sometimes you have to turn your back on obvious jokes about Uranus.

ha ha), and then I woke up to find that the hideous screeching and honking sound was not coming from any engines at all, but from the loudspeakers outside the hut. Yep, it was our friendly wake-up call.

At least it didn't turn Hut Four into zombies again. They were just normal fat kids groaning and farting and trying to get out of bed by snuggling further under the covers. And then the door flew open and a gale of dead leaves and sleet blew in, along with three of the goons, who ran around screaming, 'Raus! Raus! Schnell! Schnell!' At first I thought that Raus and Schnell must be two of the fat kids, but then I figured out that it was just special goon talk for 'Out' and 'Quickly'.

The next thing I knew, a goon had pulled off the flimsy blanket that was the only thing protecting me from the horror of the outside world and hurled me onto the floor.

'OUTSIDE IN TWO MINUTES OR BREAKFAST WILL BE CANCELLED!' screamed another.

That was enough to make me get dressed double quick. It certainly helped that the orange tracksuits only took a few seconds to put on. What didn't help was having a goon shouting in my face all the time. There's nothing better designed to slow you down than having someone yell, 'Hurry up!' in your ear.

It was still dark outside, and cold enough to freeze the snot in your nose. We formed a line, and then we had to jog towards the gates of the camp. Halfway there we slowed down and picked up a carrot from a tin bucket.

That was breakfast.

Now, I've never really understood carrots. As far as I can tell they don't taste of anything at all. That is actually not a bad thing, for a vegetable. It would be much worse if a carrot tasted of something like broccoli, cabbage or cauliflower, like broccoli, cabbages and cauliflowers do. But what I don't get are those people who munch on raw carrots as if they were apples or cakes or something, and claim to actually like them.

But I was starving, so I ate my carrot and, may the God of Donuts forgive me, I finished it right down to the stumpy little bit of green stalk at the end. As we ate, we continued our jog. We were accompanied not just by the goons, but by their little sausage guard dogs:* not Gustav himself,

* Or should that be guard sausage dogs? Or sausage dog guards? Who knows. Who cares.

126

who was too grand for mere guard duty, but his equally nasty comrades. Like I said, they were as evil as orcs, and kept on snarling and nipping at our ankles, which made me quite pleased about their stumpy legs. If anyone had managed to create a race of long-legged sausage dogs, then they'd no doubt have tucked into our ample backsides, the ruthless monsters.

We jogged through the gates and J-Man moved up to my side.

'Don't drop behind,' he said. 'If you do, the dogs will fall on you like wolves.'

I sped up a little.

Soon we were in among the trees. All around me, fat kids were sucking asthmatically for breath, dogs were yapping, goons were shouting. My body couldn't decide if it was too hot or too cold. I was sweating and shivering.

'H-h-how long do we have to run for?' I gasped in the general direction of J-Man.

'TILL YOU DROP!' screamed a goon, who'd overheard me.

Finally, just as I thought I could jog no more, the head goon yelled out, 'Stop!' We were in a clearing. I promptly fell to my knees and, I'm sorry to say, puked. You know how normally there are a few bits of carrot in your sick, and you always point to them and say in a supposedly humorous way, 'I don't know how carrots get in sick. I don't even eat carrots,' etc., etc.? Well, this time what came out of me was 99.9 per cent carrot, with a tiny little bit of normal sick in it.

I'd have pointed this out to one of my companions, but they were all leaving their own chunky orange puddles, so there didn't seem to be much point. I suppose it's the beauty of keeping a diary – you can write stuff like that in it, otherwise it would all just go to waste.

When I'd stopped being sick I looked around. There were about thirty kids here – the occupants of my hut, plus half a dozen others. There was also a pick-up truck that had arrived before us. And standing next to it, wearing a cowboy hat and a pair of mirrored aviator sunglasses, was the deeply unpleasant sight of Boss Skinner.

Once we'd all stopped vomiting, the other goons shepherded us over to the truck. Then Boss Skinner made a speech in his whispering mode so we had to strain to hear his words.

'For the benefit of those of you who haven't done this before, I want teams of two. One pick, one shovel. The pick guy picks, the shovel guy shovels. You find worms. The worms go in the bucket. You fill up the bucket, then we go back to camp. You don't fill up the bucket, you

sleep here tonight. Anyone runs, we set the dogs on you. Anyone talks, we set the dogs on you. Anyone digs too slow, we set the dogs on you. Got any questions? If you do, we set the dogs on you.'

We divided into pairs, and got out tools from the back of the truck. I ended up with Ernesto Gogol, the spotty, weaselly kid with the sharp teeth. I had the impression that nobody else wanted to pair up with him.

Or with me, for that matter.

I guessed that having a partner new to the pick-and-shovel routine was bad news. Anyway, Gogol got the glamour job – the picking – while I did the grunt work – the shovelling.

So he hacked away with the pick, then I shovelled with the shovel, putting the loose soil to one side. Then we both went through the soil looking for worms. Luckily it was quite a good place for worms. Long, thin, slimy ones; short, fat, juicy ones. Think I'm gonna . . .

No, I wasn't that hungry. Yet.

After an hour we had half filled our bucket, and the worms were getting scarcer. I was dog-tired and we were all pretty grubby by then from all the scrabbling about in the mud. It was also freezing. And my back ached, along with all the other bits of me, except, possibly, my earlobes. And although it was tough enough to make everything hurt, the work wasn't quite hard enough to keep us warm, and the sweat from the run had seeped out to meet the drenching rain working its way in.

Just then I heard a sort of magical music. A tinkling, dream-like sound. In my befuddled state, I thought for a moment that I'd died and gone to heaven, and the music was the strumming of the angels' harps as the pearly gates opened up for me, and a saintly baker was offering me a plate of golden donuts – but, you know, the sort of gold you can eat.

And then I realized what it was. Somewhere, away through the woods, there was a road, and on that road an ice-cream van had parked and was playing its tune, calling out to the starving and the wretched, offering salvation in a cone or on a stick.

Instantly, all the heads that had been bowed towards the earth and the worms therein shot up.

'Nobody moves,' came the deathly quiet voice of Boss Skinner. 'Or I set . . .'

But it was too much for one fat kid. It was Flo, the dough-faced boy. Anyway, we all heard a strangled cry and sensed the earth shudder, and the blimp got to his feet.

J-Man yelled, 'Noooooooo!' but it was too late. The siren call of the ice-cream van was too strong. Dong tried to tackle him, but Flo burst through his grasp and was off, pounding through the clearing and towards the trees.

I looked at Boss Skinner. His face was blank. He spat on the ground, and then hissed out of the side of his mouth, 'Release the hounds.'

The goon who had been holding the slavering sausage dogs let them go. The little devils were already straining, and burst away like guided missiles.

But Flo was moving well for a fat boy, and was already quite close to the trees. If he could

reach them he might be in with a chance – the
undergrowth was quite deep and tangled in
there, and the stumpy-legged little dogs might
not be able to keep up with him.

'Go on, you can make it, Flo,' J-Man said, and
the cry was taken up.

'Go on!'

'Run!'

'Run!'

'Run!'

He was almost there, but then I heard the *ker-chick-ker* that could only be the sound of a pump-action paintball shotgun being cocked. I saw Boss Skinner aim and fire, and a deadly red butterfly opened up on Flo's back. He was down, and the pack reached him, snarling and snapping.

The next thing I knew I was running to help him. J-Man cried out weakly, 'No, Donut, there's nothing you can do . . .' but then, when he saw that I wasn't stopping, he joined me. We reached Flo together, and tried to pull the hounds off him. Suddenly we were surrounded by a mass of other kids, with the goons pushing and shoving their way towards us.

'Heel,' came a quiet but sinister voice.

Instantly the dogs backed off.

'Now, take these vermin to the cooler.'

The other goons bundled us into the back of the pick-up truck. Flo was whimpering. J-Man looked like he wanted to murder someone.

'Now see what you've done,' he hissed at me as we bumped over the rough track on the way back to the camp.

'What's this cooler like?'

Flo moaned again.

'You'll soon find out,' said J-Man.

And I did.

We had a lesson on 'Irony' last term in English. It's when the actual meaning of a word or phrase is different to the literal meaning. So, for example, if you say something stupid, and I say, 'Well done, Einstein,' that's being ironic. It's a lot like sarcasm, except . . . er, well, it's a lot like sarcasm. Anyway, it turned out that the cooler was not an ironic term.

'It' was actually several cold storage units under the kitchen block. I was kicked into one by Badwig, who then slammed the door and bolted it shut. J-Man was in another box next to me, and Flo was in one on the other side. There wasn't enough room to stand up or lie down, so I had to sit hunched against the wall. And did I mention it was cold? Really cold? Well, it was. And worst of all, there was a metal rail running along the roof, and hanging from the rail by vicious-looking hooks were carcasses. I don't know what they were. Probably piglets, judging by the size. Skinned piglets. Dead, obviously. I guessed that they were the origin of the nasty meat on the plates at dinner time.

Dinner.

I was famished.

I thought about gnawing at the raw, chilled bodies hanging from the roof. But that would have meant that I was a monster. And I wasn't a monster. Not yet.

After five bleak, shivery minutes, I heard a pounding on the wall.

'You OK, Donut?' came the deep voice of J-Man.

'Nope.'

'Check on Flo, will you?'

I slapped on the other wall. 'Hey, Florian, you OK?'

All I heard was a quiet sobbing. At least he was still alive.

They left us in there for three or four hours.

I found a mouldy potato on the floor and tried
to keep warm by bouncing it off the wall.

Then I ate the potato.

By the time they came to drag me out my

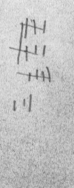

legs weren't working properly. J-Man and
Flo were in the same poor shape. The goons
frog-marched us back to the hut, dogs yapping
again at our ankles.

I was starting to really hate those dogs.

The others gathered round as we lay in a
heap on the floor. We'd missed dinner, but
they'd saved us a few scraps. Some carrots
(of course), a couple of cups of cold gruel,
some of the slabs of meat. I took the gruel and
a carrot, but turned down the meat. I hadn't
liked the look of the things I'd seen in the
cooler.

In front of them all, J-Man said to me,
'Donut, you did a brave thing, trying to help
Flo. You're one of us now.'

The others murmured their agreement.
At lights-out, Flo waddled over and offered

to let me sleep with his cuddly beetle, but I declined.

It wasn't a bad end to a day of horror piled upon horror.

DONUT COUNT:

Hey, you do the math.

Wednesday 4 April

Same routine this morning. A carrot for breakfast, long jog out to the clearing in the forest, dig for worms.

'Why are we digging for worms?' I asked J-Man during a carrot break.

He shrugged heavily. 'Some say it's to sell to fishermen. Some say they mash them up and turn them into that meat they give us. But I say the goons don't need no reason to make us work. They just do it because they can.'

'That's enough mouth from you, boy,' yelled one of the goons, a big man with a bull-neck called Spanner.* He was in Boss Skinner's role for today, and you could see that he actually wanted one of us to run so that he could put a paintball round into some kid's face.

After a couple of hours of wearisome worm work, we jogged back to have lunch. Guess what? Gruel. And a carrot. I was starting to hate carrots, the way someone dying of the plague might hate rats. And boils.

We had a stroll around the perimeter fence after lunch. Dong, the Chinese kid, was there

---

* I don't mean that his bull-neck was called Spanner. The name belonged to all of him, almost certainly including his neck. I mean, it would be fairly stupid of him to have a separate name for his neck, but then he was fairly stupid, which you could tell from the way he kept accidentally spitting on his own feet.

with us, plus Igor, who loomed over us all in his friendly ogre-ish way. Every few metres there was a sign attached to the wire saying:

**ELECTRIC FENCE:
10,000 VOLTS
DO NOT TOUCH!**

We came to a large section where the wire was replaced by a tall wall of corrugated iron, hiding what lay beyond it.

'What's through there?' I asked.

J-Man shrugged.

'What we can't get, so best not to know.'

I looked into his face, but he wasn't giving away anything else, so I changed the subject.

'How do people stand it here?'

'How do we stand it? You make it sound like we got a choice.'

'But why don't the kids get in touch with their parents, tell them what it's like?'

'How? You know they got no phones, no internet, no way of getting a message out, unless Igor knocks one of them pigeons out of the air with a butt-blast, and fastens a note to its leg. And anyways, the parents don't care. They dump us all here just to get rid of us. My dad's a lawyer. My mom's a lawyer. You think they want my fat ass hanging round the apartment all day during school vacation? I don't match the curtains.'

'But this place . . . it's barbaric.'

'Sure is. But it works. We all go back thinner, don't we?'

'They don't look like they're losing much weight,' I said, pointing my chin in the direction of a group of the fattest kids. I recognized them as the ones J-Man had called the Lardies.

'Yeah, the Lardies. Like I said, there ain't no famine where there ain't someone getting fat, no sir.'

One of the Lardies saw me looking over and caught my eye. I felt a stab of apprehension, as though someone had punched me in the guts. I usually feel this just before someone punches me in the guts. Actually, my school is the sort of school where the bullying takes the form of teasing, mickey-taking, humiliation on an epic scale, etc., etc., rather than actual punching and kicking. Most of the punches and kicks I've had, in the guts and elsewhere, have been delivered by my sisters, the dreaded Ruby and Ella.

But this was different. This was a big, tough-looking kid, who was giving me the stare – the stare that says, *You, yep, you, I'm thinking seriously about punching you in the face, so you may as well start crying now.*

And he was coming towards me, his hands already formed into fists. For an overweight kid I'm quite fast, and I did think about running away. But my new friends were here and it wouldn't look great. Especially if I also started crying. That kind of thing can really destroy your reputation in an institution like Camp Fatso. So I stood my ground and tried hard not to wet my pants.

'What you looking at?' said the kid. He had a buzz cut, and now he was close enough, I could see that he had homemade tattoos on his knuckles: LOVE on one hand and HAET on the other. OK, so I was dealing with a dyslexic psychopath.

'Me? Nothing.'

'You saying I'm nothing?'

It was the most obvious trap in the world. Obvious and unavoidable. I sensed some more of the Lardies looming up behind me. I opened my mouth, hoping something might come out that would save me from a beating – but it was a bit like when you search in your pockets for change so you can buy a donut, even though you absolutely know there's nothing in there except for a snotty hankie, some old sweet papers, and a fluff-covered something, the origins of which you are too afraid to speculate about.

'Get lost, Gilbert,' said J-Man, rescuing me.

Gilbert.

Not Spike, or Killer, or Razor, but Gilbert.

What else could I do but snigger?

Bad move.

One of Gilbert's fists – the one with HAET on the knuckles – opened. I thought for a second that it meant he wasn't going to hit me after all. Maybe he was going to shake hands. Then he brought the hand up and sent it open-palmed towards my face. It turned out that I wasn't even worth a punch. I was going to get a slap.

The slap never arrived.

On my right side, J-Man started to move, but he was too slow. There was a blur, and a flurry, and suddenly the tattooed oaf was face-down on the floor. It was Dong, who had appeared on my left, his face as passive and inscrutable as ever. I tried to replay what had happened in slow motion in my head. I think Dong had caught the other kid's wrist and then performed some sort of ninja move, but it really was too quick for the human eye to take in.

And then I was aware that it wasn't just me and Dong and J-Man together, but the whole of Hut Four, who were now confronting an angry mob of Lardies.

Another Lardy stepped forward. There was something weirdly pie-like about his head, although maybe that was just a hallucination brought on by the carrots I'd been eating. This time it was the huge Igor who went to meet him. Igor gave him a standard school-yard shove in the chest – the kind of thing you see a hundred times every day – but this was delivered with such power that now a second Lardy was on the floor.

Two–nil to Hut Four!

And then it looked like it was going to turn really ugly, like a massive sumo brawl. I thought about those nature documentaries where elephant seals fight, whacking each other with their monstrous necks and trying to get in a good old bite or three, and at the end the beach is littered with squashed pups.

But before mayhem ensued, one of the

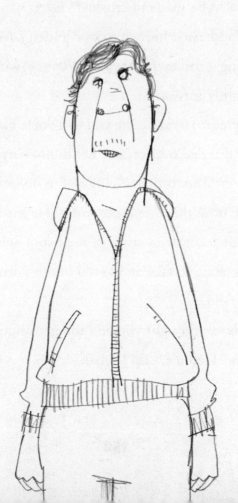

Lardies eased forward, a pleasant smile on his face. He had the beginnings of a fuzzy moustache on his top lip, and there was a general air of neatness and delicacy about him, despite his bulk. His tracksuit wasn't like ours: it seemed to be made of crushed velvet.

He addressed himself to our leader, J-Man, adopting a somewhat theatrical stance, with one leg slightly forward.

'My dear Jermaine,' he said in a voice like honey drizzled over cream. 'Let us not permit this to escalate further. Neither of us desires trouble from the, *ahem*, authorities.' He made a gesture towards a couple of the goons, who were starting to take an interest in our corner of the field.

'I always thought you and the goons got on just fine, Hercule,' said J-Man.

Hercule shook his head slowly. 'You had such promise, once,' he said in that honeyed, poisonous voice of his. And then he turned to me. 'You're the new boy, aren't you? There's always room in my organization for boys of, ah, character. And there are perks, you know. Good food. More appropriate clothing.' He stroked the thick velvet of his lapel. 'An easier life.'

'I'm happy where I am,' I said, struggling to overcome the sickening, hypnotic power of his voice.

'You keep your paws off my boys,' said J-Man.

'Do you think to threaten me, Jermaine? I've gone easy on you, on account of our old comradeship. But that leniency is now at an end. Consider that from now on your actions will have consequences.'

'You can stick your consequences where the sun don't shine,' said J-Man.

Hercule made as if to reply, then smiled sweetly, turned, and walked away with the other Lardies.

'You used to be one of those guys?' I asked.

'Yeah.'

'Why did you leave?'

'Because a kid's got to sleep at night. And there's things I won't do for an extra helping of gruel. C'mon, let's get changed, it's time for PE. And I gotta tell you, PE here ain't fun, no sir.'

So back we went to good old Hut Four, and got changed into the Camp Fatso sports kit. This should actually have been called the Camp Fatso torture kit. It consisted of an absurdly tight orange (of course) top and a pair of ludicrous micro shorts, designed *solely* to humiliate us. OK, not solely; they had an important secondary function of cutting off the blood supply to the extremities, thereby causing a long, agonizing death by gangrene.

Dough-faced Flo had tried to manufacture a bigger pair of shorts by stitching together two smaller pairs, but the outcome was like the ghastly product of some scientific experiment to create a new life form that had gone horribly wrong, and spawned a monster.

J-Man chivvied us along.

'Let's move it, guys! You know we lose dinner if we get out there late.'

So we trundled out onto the sports field, along with about fifty other Camp Fatso kids. Waiting there for us was a small, bald goon whose name, as I soon found out, was Mr Phlapp.

'Settle down now,' said Mr Phlapp, in a perfectly normal voice. It turned out that Phlapp was about the least insane adult I'd met at Camp Fatso. True, there were a couple of things that limited his skills as a PE instructor. The first was that he didn't seem to like sport very much. The second was that, instead of sport, he had a strange obsession with human pyramids. This is when you get kids to stand on each other's shoulders, each layer being smaller than the one below it, the whole forming a rough pyramid shape. It was an unpleasant and hazardous operation, especially considering the size of those taking part.

'Right, let's begin with a basic three-two-one,' said Phlapp, and soon the field was scattered with little pyramids: three kids on the bottom row, then two, then one. I was put in a group with J-Man, Dong, Flo and two fat twins from another hut, whom everyone called the Tweedles. I began on the bottom row, which was both the easiest and the hardest job. Easiest, because it required zero skill – you just had to stand there without falling over. Hardest, because you had what felt like several tons worth of fatty standing on your shoulders.

'Good work, nice shape, very pyramidical,' said Phlapp in an encouraging way. 'Now let's have a good clean dismount.'

There was quite a lot of falling, landing face-down in the mud, etc., etc., but no serious injuries.

'Excellent, time to move up to the classic four-three-two-one.'

This time round I found myself on the

second tier. I had to climb up the legs, back and shoulders of the guy beneath me – who, luckily, was the titanic Igor. To him I was as insignificant as a fly on an ox.

I didn't mind the second tier. It wasn't high enough for my fear of heights to kick in, and the strain wasn't as bad as being at the bottom. But it still isn't exactly how I'd choose to spend my leisure hours. Especially not as the wind and rain had begun to pick up.

'OK, one more and we'll call it a day,' said Phlapp. 'And let's make it the majestic five-four-three-two-one. You, young man, the new boy, what's your name?'

'Me, sir? Dermot.'

'Why don't you have a go at the top?'

'Er . . .'

Obviously, there were at least nine reasons why I shouldn't 'have a go at the top'.

1. I was a rank beginner at the art of the human pyramid.
2. I was afraid of heights.
3. I was a bit of a klutz. Not as bad as some of my nerdy friends back at school, such as Renfrew and Spam, who basically couldn't be trusted to tie their own shoelaces without stabbing themselves in the eye, but you wouldn't want to let me hold your priceless Ming vase.
4. I didn't want to.
5. It was now really, really rainy and windy.
6. It (i.e. the formation of the human pyramid) was a truly stupid activity at the best of times.

7. I mean, a human pyramid? Why . . . ?

8. OK, I'm struggling. Maybe there were just seven reasons.

9. Did I mention that I really didn't want to do it?

But they were all there waiting for me. They were the cake, and I was the cherry, so I began to clamber up the enormous, but still uncapped, human pyramid that had miraculously formed before my very eyes.

Yes, it was the Great Pyramid of Fat Geezers!

It wasn't just my crew any more, but other kids I didn't know, so I had to keep saying, 'Excuse me,' and, 'Sorry about that,' and, 'Ooops!' whenever I put my foot or hand in the wrong place – and it turns out that almost everywhere is the wrong place when one human being is climbing over another.

But it was going OK. I was up to the penultimate tier – the one with two fat kids. I was quite pleased to see that it was the Tweedle twins, who you'd have thought would be used to working as a team.

And then I made the fatal mistake of looking down. I hadn't quite grasped how high up it was going to be. It felt like I was on top of the Eiffel Tower. An Eiffel Tower made out of fat people.

Phlapp was looking up as I looked down.

'Keep at it, lad, you're doing fine.'

I don't know why, but I always find encouragement discouraging. It means the person doing the encouraging thinks I'm about to fail – otherwise why bother encouraging me?

But I didn't want to fail. I wanted to complete
the pyramid, to form a perfect geometrical
shape here amid the horrors of Camp Fatso. It
would be a blow struck on behalf of, er, human
pyramids everywhere!

So I gritted my teeth and climbed on. Right
foot on Tweedledum's left thigh, left foot on
Tweedledee's right. Now the shoulder. I was
still holding onto Dee and Dum's hair with my
hands . . . I just had to let go and stand fully
erect.

I stood.

I'd done it.

Phlapp beamed proudly. Kids around the field
began to clap.

And I could see for miles. See over the
fence. See the woods beyond and, further out,
fields and roads and freedom. And in the other

direction I could see over the blank wall of corrugated iron. What I saw there astonished me.

It was another camp.

And it was full of girls.

Girls playing rounders and netball. Girls skipping and laughing. And even though the rain was lashing into our faces on this side of the wall, over there the sun was shining.

So that's what J-Man had meant.

Then I felt a wobble. I glanced down again. Phlapp was somehow unsatisfied with the positioning of one of the boys on the bottom tier. There was a kink where there should have been a straight line. He was fiddling, prodding, pulling, trying to get back to that state of geometric perfection he craved. But I knew that it was insanity. Even after my short

acquaintance with the human pyramid, I knew
that it is folly to mess with the structure once
it is up.

And yes, the inevitable was happening. The
line kinked more, then buckled. One of the
bottom-tier kids went down on one knee and
the whole edifice began to crumble. Tier by
tier, the pyramid collapsed. Poor Phlapp tried
vainly to shore it up, but it was futile.

And fatal.

At the last moment he seemed to realize the
peril he was in, and he turned and began to
run. But it was too late. I was already falling.
I'm not sure who screamed louder, me or him.

And then I landed right on top of him with
a sickening crunch, with a certain amount of
added splat, crushing him into the mud, like an
elephant sitting on a quail's egg.

It hurt, but not that much, as the soft mud
provided a certain amount of cushioning. As did
my in-built air-bags.

I picked myself up. The crowd around us was
silent for a second or two. And then someone –
Flo, I think – said, 'Jeepers, you've killed him …'

And suddenly the other goons were there, and people were shouting in my face, including Boss Skinner and Badwig. I heard the words 'deliberate attack' and 'assassination attempt' and I tried weakly to protest. 'I didn't mean to kill him,' I said, which made me sound like the most pathetic murderer in history.

And then, to my relief, I heard a groan, and Phlapp pushed himself up onto his elbows. 'Accident . . .' he said, his voice as frail and feeble as a dying daddy-longlegs.

Boss Skinner's black eyes bored into me. 'Your lucky day, boy,' he whispered, as if he'd been hoping that Phlapp really had died, just so he could inflict suitable retribution on me.

Half an hour later the ambulance arrived to take Phlapp away.

Nothing very interesting happened during the rest of the day.

Dinner was gruel.

In the evening we lay on our bunks whilst Igor played his harmonica. I say 'played' but I really mean 'blew' as you wouldn't call any of the sounds that came out of it 'music'.

I was glad when it was lights-out. Sometimes the oblivion of sleep is all you can hope for.

DONUT COUNT:

If we include the ones I dreamed of that night, then 764. If not, then zero.

Thursday 5 April

This morning the camp was all abuzz about the squishing incident. A couple of guys clapped me on the back during the worm dig. No one seemed to believe that it was an accident. I decided to let them think what they wanted to think.

I'd been doing a lot of thinking myself – mainly about what I'd seen from the top of the human pyramid. The girls' camp looked a lot nicer than ours. The buildings were new, and there was what appeared to be a gym and a swimming pool. I talked to J–Man about it during a carrot break.

'Yeah, the girls' camp's what they let the outside world see. Remember the DVDs and all that publicity material? That was all shot in the girls' camp.'

'But the girls . . . the ones I saw, they weren't all, er . . .'

'Fat? Like us? That's right, boy. They call that side of the institution Camp Fitso, and they've got girls of all shapes and sizes in there.'

'And I didn't see any dogs or goons . . .'

'Why'd they need dogs or goons? That place is paradise, I hear. They get three good meals a day. Sure, it's healthy stuff, but it's real, hot food. Risotto and steamed fish and fruit smoothies for dessert, and, well, I don't know what else. Who'd want to escape from that, huh?'

And that's when the plan started to form in my head. And it was only in my head for a second before it came right out of my lips.

'I reckon I could dig under the wall, and get into the girls' camp. Then I could walk right out of there.'

J-Man nodded.

'You ain't the first to have that idea. They dig that wall down deep. And even if you get under it, if someone spots you in the girls' camp, they send some goons over there. And if you make it out of the camp, then one of the patrols pick you up for sure. And then they lock you in the cooler and throw away the key, yes sir.'

'But if I could get out, then I could tell the world about what's going on here.'

'The world won't believe you, boy. Now let's dig some more of these worms before Boss Skinner fires off that pop gun of his.'

Even though I'd only been in Camp Fatso for a few days it already seemed like I was in the routine. But then, in the afternoon, something happened that turned my new world upside down. Turned it upside down, kicked it in the pants, slapped its face and poked it in the eye.

So, the siren went for afternoon PE. It was generally assumed that one of the goons would take charge, probably just continuing the great tradition of human pyramid building established by Mr Phlapp. And that seemed to be working out: two low-ranking goons got us to line up for the afternoon roll-call.

I was in the second row, and was in the

middle of a donut daydream. Most of my waking moments (as well as pretty much all of my old-fashioned night-time dreaming) were now taken up with donut fantasies. This one involved a giant bouncy donut castle, and every time I landed I took a bite out of it. But as with nearly all my fantasies, it started to go wrong. I suppose it should have been obvious, but the biting business had the predictable effect of deflating the bouncy donut castle, so it was shrinking underneath me, adding a frantic, eat-it-while-it-lasts vibe to the fantasy.

Then I realized that someone had started talking to us. Well, not so much talking as yelling. There'd been plenty of yelling at Camp Fatso, but this was a yell that was both familiar and terrible.

I peered around the fat head in front of me

and there was the baleful form of . . .

MR FRICKER!!!!!

He had on his Terminator hands – bare metal with rivets and bolts, like pieces of some infernal engine.

'. . . I understand that things have been pretty sloppy around here,' he was saying, I mean shouting. 'But things will change. You can say goodbye to the human pyramid. I've scoured the world looking for healthful activities, stimulating to the body and mind. Exercises which—'

And then Fricker stopped. He stopped because he'd seen me. A shadow passed over his face – a shadow shaped something like an eagle, something like the shape that the feeling hate would make if it were made out of shadow. A little motor whirred in his mechanical right hand, and the fingers closed tightly in a sort

of hamster-strangling way. Had he forgotten
that we'd bonded (sort of) over the choking
disaster? That I'd saved him from the mother of
all wedgies? Had his primitive mind bundled
up the idea of me and his painful humiliation?
Sometimes, with grown-ups, you just don't
know.

'You!' he said, after a few awkward seconds.
He tried to point, but his hand was stuck in

hamster-strangling mode. He had to use the other hand to straighten out one finger, and aimed it at my eyeball. 'Yes, you, Millicent, out here.'*

Gulping, I pushed my way forward.

'You can help me demonstrate today's World Sport. Peruvian shoe-throwing. Comes from the highlands of Peru. Played by the ancient Aztecs—'

'Incas, surely, sir,' I said, forgetting, in the heat of the moment, to keep my STUPID MOUTH SHUT.

'Run!' commanded Fricker, ignoring my interruption.

'What?'

---

* One of Mr Fricker's little jokes was to misremember my name in various unpleasantly feminine forms.

'Run!'

'Where?'

'Away, boy, away!'

So I started to run, heading roughly in the
direction of the perimeter fence. I glanced back
over my shoulder, in time to see Mr Fricker

stoop, pull off his trainer, take aim, and hurl it at me with the skill and power of an international-grade Peruvian (Inca or Aztec) shoe-thrower. The shoe hit me square between the shoulder blades.

'Right,' yelled Fricker. 'That's it. You've got the rules. And anyone who misses, or shows a lack of appropriate Aztec vigour, becomes the Peruvian.'

So for the next half-hour I was chased around the field while fat kids threw their shoes at me. At the end we played a subtle variation, whereby the Peruvian is thrown at the shoes.

Now, the thing about being hit with shoes is that it's quite painful, but doesn't do too much actual bodily harm. Otherwise I suppose it would have been developed further as a weapon of war, and you'd have had knights fighting jousts with fearsome shoe-maces, and battleships firing broadsides of kitten-heels, and perhaps armour-piercing sandals for anti-tank use. It also helped that the guys of Hut Four were on my side. They had to throw their shoes as well, but they did it in the gentlest possible fashion, and they also formed a sort of protective wall around me, and also discouraged the others from hurling their shoes with too much force. Nevertheless it was one of the most gruesome thirty minutes of my life, and as each trainer thudded into the back of my head, or my legs, or bounced off my belly, I silently cursed the evil Fricker.

'Why's that guy hate you so much, Donut?' J-Man asked when it was all over. 'You run into him before?'

'Could say. He's the PE teacher at my school.'

'Seems kinda weird, him turning up here like that.'

'I realized a long time ago, J-Man, that it's weird when something weird doesn't happen.'

'I hear you, Donut. I hear you.'

After a delicious supper of caviar, roast suckling pig, chips, more chips, chocolate éclairs and donuts (gruel, actually), I was more or less carried to bed by the guys. I was battered and bruised, but not beaten.

'I need to get over the wall,' I said to J-Man, as he tucked me in and fluffed my pillow.

'No, kid,' he said. 'You don't. What you gotta do is tough it out, like the rest of us saps.'

DONUT COUNT:

NO
donuts

Friday 6 April

Now I've got to know them all a bit better, I
think I should give a more detailed sketch of
the other guys in Hut Four, as it's not really fair
just to think of Flo as the dough-faced beetle
geek, and Dong as the silent Ninja, although that
actually does kind of sum them up.

J-Man

I don't need to say much more about J-Man.
He's black, cool as a panther (but fat as a bear,

so you've got two *Jungle Book* characters for the price of one), wise, brave, loyal and strong. In a nutshell (a giant nutshell), my hero.

Florian Frost (Flo)

Flo is a tender-hearted soul. Unlike J-Man, I'm not convinced that he is a genius. He does seem to know a lot about beetles. And his only joke is a beetle joke. He 'did' his beetle joke for me on my second day at the camp. He approached me with a matchbox. Inside were two odd-looking, long-nosed beetles.

'Weevils,' he said, avoiding eye contact as usual. Well, avoiding eye contact with me, that is. He was perfectly good at keeping eye contact with the weevils. 'You have to choose one.'

'What do you mean, choose one? I'm not going to eat it, if that's what you mean.'

'No. I wouldn't let you eat one. Just pick your favourite.'

I looked around at the other Hut Four guys. They were all trying not to laugh.

'OK, I'll pick that one,' I said, pointing at one of them. They looked identical.

'Ha ha,' said Flo. 'Incorrect. You picked the big one.'

'So? Why is that wrong?'

'Because you should have picked the lesser of two beetles.'

'What?'

'Oh, I got it wrong, I think. I mean, you should always choose the lesser of two weevils. You see, it sounds like "two evils". People say that. They do. They say you should always choose the lesser of two evils. But I did it with weevils. It's a joke. About weevils.'

Then he got a bit over-emotional, and J-Man had to comfort him, while he rocked on the floor cuddling his fluffy beetle.

So that's Flo.

Dong

Don't know what to say about Dong, because he still doesn't speak any English, except for the 'Hello, old chap, delighted to make your acquaintance' line. It's quite hard not to see him as a Man of Mystery, but I wonder if I was trapped in the Chinese version of Camp Fatso, which is probably called something much more Chinese, like Camp of the Sleeping Overweight Dragon, then maybe they'd all see me as a Man of Mystery too, like James Bond or Harry Potter, even though I'd still be the same old Donut. Anyway, because of his special ninja powers,

Dong doesn't seem to suffer as much as the rest of us. He probably spent years training in a Tibetan monastery, learning how to put up with all kinds of privations. Although I guess that then he wouldn't be such a fatty.

Igor

Igor is the surprise package of Hut Four. Looking at him, you'd naturally assume that he's a borderline idiot, i.e. on the borderline between idiot and complete idiot. Not only is he totally huge, which people irrationally associate with being unintelligent, but he also looks a bit thick, in a drooling, blank-eyed way, which people also, and rather less irrationally, associate with being unintelligent. But yet again, it seems that appearances are deceptive.

The other evening I was lying in my bunk

trying to imagine that I was on a beautiful
tropical island, being served chilled drinks in
a coconut shell by the fair Umbilica, Queen
of the Zabamba people. (I should say that the
drink was not coconut flavoured, because I
don't like coconuts. It was some sort of fruit
juice known only to the island, tasting of
lime and mango. Or maybe pineapple and
pomegranate. Something good, anyway.) Like I
said before, all my fantasies are haunted by the
ghosts of bad things, but in this one I'd carefully
put the bad things off into the future so I could
enjoy swinging in my hammock and drinking
my delicious drink. (The bad thing, by the way,
was that I was going to have to marry Queen
Umbilica when I grew up, but only for one
day, after which I was to be sacrificed to the
Zabamba gods by being thrown into a volcano.

But, like I said, that was miles in the future.)

Anyway, I was rudely ripped from my daydream by the looming figure of Igor.

'Do you play chess?' he rumbled.

Normally he was almost as mute as Dong.

'Yeah. Sort of,' I replied.

It turned out that Igor had whittled a set of chess pieces from candles (white pieces) and some unspecified brown matter (black pieces). The board was chalked out on the bare wooden planks of the floor.

I have to say that Igor's whittling skills were, at best, just OK, so when the pieces were lined up it didn't look so much like a great medieval battle about to take place, with kings and knights and castles and whatnot, as like zombies versus apocalyptic mutants.

Now, one of the key facts about me is that

in almost every area of human endeavour, I'm better than all the people who are rubbish at whatever activity it is we're talking about, but not as good as the people who are, well, good at it. So, with football, I'm better than all my useless mates, but not anywhere near as good as the kids in the school team. The rule applies to chess, but given that most people are rubbish at chess, I usually end up winning.

Well, not against Igor. I'd assumed that I'd wipe the floor with him. In the first game he beat me in two moves.

'Fool's mate,' he said, and flicked my king over so hard his head fell off (the king's, not Igor's — it would take more than a flick to decapitate Igor. You'd need an axe for sure. Or a guillotine).

Fair enough. I'd been complacent. I wouldn't make that mistake again.

The next game lasted four moves.

'Scholar's mate,' he said.

After that I got better, and after six games
I was lasting long enough to avoid total
humiliation. But he still beat me every time.

So, it seems that Igor is not just big. He's *deep*.

Ernesto Gogol

Ernesto is the odd one out in the hut. Firstly,
as I've said before, he isn't fat, just unhealthy.
He looks like he's been brought up in the dark,
like some creature you'd find under a stone.
He's always making writhing movements, like a
maggot. And those scary pointed teeth – what
to make of those? He sometimes tries to be
friendly, offering to share his portion of gruel,
but he's also incredibly sensitive to any kind
of insult. One day he offered me a bite of his

carrot. I'd had enough carrot, and not enough of anything else, so I said no thanks. Maybe I didn't say it in my most polite voice, but I didn't say, 'No, you evil, pointy-toothed freak, I wouldn't eat your carrot if it was the last edible morsel on earth, because you've gnawed at it with your disgusting teeth, and so you can stick it up your nose.' Although that was, basically, what I was thinking.

The little demon seemed almost to burst into flames. He hissed like a cat, and I noticed for the first time that his nails were also long and pointed, and black.

'So, Gogol food not good enough for the Donut, is it?' he sizzled. 'Frightened of a little bit of Gogol spit, is he? Well, one day Donut will be frightened. Very frightened. And all will bow down before Gogol, and Gogol will not forget who was kind and who was unkind. That day Gogol will—'

'Shut up, Ernesto,' said J-Man, and he did, thank heavens.

Traditionally, of course, there's always a traitor in every group, a secret baddy, a sneak, a Gollum, and if Hut Four was going to have an evil traitor it would definitely be him.

So that's the hut.

And I hope that tonight is the last time I shall see any of them again.

You see, I finally persuaded J-Man to help me go over the wall into the girls' camp, using the human pyramid we were practising before Fricker arrived. We're going to try it tonight, after lights-out.

Naturally I didn't include Ernesto Gogol in

the plan, what with him almost certainly being
a freakish, pointy-toothed traitor and all.

DONUT COUNT:

Well, zero, of course. But for once I don't care,
because I'm getting out of this hellhole.

Sunday 8 April

If it hadn't been a totally rubbish thing to say for at least a hundred, and possibly a thousand, years, what I'd be saying right now is, 'Woe is me. Woe is me, I say again.'

As you can see, two days have gone by since my last entry on the toilet roll. And am I now at home, belly full, body warm, mind at ease?

Nope.

This is what happened.

The camp was in darkness by 10 p.m on Friday.

The hut guys all knew what was happening, except for Gogol. I waited until his tell-tale snoring began – a pigletty sound of exactly the kind you'd expect to come out of a traitor, sneak, etc., etc. Or a piglet.

Quiet as giant mice, we crept from our beds and out of the hut. I'd been monitoring the movements of the guards for the past couple of nights. Goons with dogs did a patrol of the grounds on the hour, and at thirty minutes past. That would have given us half an hour to get over the wall, which should have been a piece of cake. Oh, cake, cakey, dear old cakey . . . *caaaaaaaaake* . . .

Where was I? Oh yes, but it wasn't that easy. At quarter past and quarter to, the goons in the watchtowers would turn their searchlights on and sweep the compound.

This meant that we had fifteen minutes max. But even that couldn't be relied on. Sometimes the goons in the towers would do an extra sweep, out of boredom, I guess. And if we were caught in the searchlight, then it wouldn't just mean the cooler: those automatic paintball cannons they had up there would rain red destruction on our heads.

Dong had some black boot polish, and we all smeared our faces with the foul stuff, which added very much to the excitement of the whole thing. Except for J-Man, that is, who had a natural advantage for night-time adventures of this sort.

Even though it was my plan, it was J-Man who took the lead, of course. But I was incredibly proud of all the guys. True, I was taking the biggest risk, and would definitely be the hero if this was ever made into a multimillion-pound movie, although it would be quite hard to find an actor who had sufficient charisma to play me, and who was also quite fat.

Anyway, off we slipped, moving between the pools of deepest darkness formed by the shadows of the huts. It was about five hundred metres, and we had to be careful, so it took a good ten minutes for us to reach the imposing, ominous majesty of the wall.

There were only five of us, so we were going to have to improvise a hitherto never attempted and highly unstable two-one-one-one pyramid. In fact it was really more of a human Leaning Tower of Pisa, if we're being accurate. The only way to pull it off was for the whole human edifice to lean against the wall for stability.

This is how we were arranged:

ME

J-MAN

D O N G

FLO - IGOR

I had to ascend last. It was both easier and harder than my previous efforts. Harder, in that it was pitch black, so I couldn't see where I was putting my hands and feet. Easier, in that the human pyramid was reclining against the wall, so I wasn't climbing straight up.

And somehow, despite the strain and effort, each of my comrades managed to say an encouraging word as I climbed over them.

'A pawn can take a queen, Donut: be that pawn.'

'If you find any interesting beetles, keep them for me.'

'Hello, old chap, delighted to make your acquaintance.'

And then I was scrambling up J-Man. He said not a word. We'd grown pretty close and I guess he was all gummed up with emotion.

So, with a lot of huffing and puffing, I managed to get up onto J-Man's shoulders. The top of the wall was just out of reach. I was going to have to jump for it.

Let me tell you, jumping when you're on top of a swaying pyramid of straining fat kids is not easy. But just as my feet were on the shoulders of the residents of Hut Four, I knew that their hopes were on mine, and I put everything into one last effort.

I leaped.

Not quite like a panther. More like a frightened pig. But still, it was definitely a leap and not merely a jump. My hands just reached the top of the wall. I sensed that the pyramid had crumbled beneath and behind me, heard the muffled cries as my friends fell. But I was there. I heaved, I scrambled, I made it to the top, and threw one leg over. The wall was made of corrugated iron, and it cut into me like a knife: this was not a place that I wanted to stay for very long.

And then the fatal flaw in my plan revealed itself: there was no matching human pyramid on the girls' side. But there was no going back now, and no sense in hesitating. I dangled down by my arms, swayed, gulped, and let go.

It was a drop of five metres – enough to do some serious damage if you landed on something hard, like concrete or a really tricky

maths puzzle, but I was counting on a soft

landing, because of all the rain, sleet and general boggy misery we'd had at Camp Fatso.

And my landing was quite soft, but only because I landed in the huge arms of perhaps the only person at Camp Fitso who could have caught me without being thoroughly squashed.

'Pfumpf,' said the monstrous form of . . .

LUDMILLA!!!*

'Great way to spoil a perfectly good midnight feast.'

But it wasn't Ludmilla who said that (it couldn't be, because Ludmilla mainly said, 'Pfumpf' – hence her name). And nor was it me, as I was still too utterly flabbergasted at this turn

---

* Actually, 'monstrous' is a little unfair. Inside Ludmilla's massive form were some pretty huge bones. But inside those was a heart that was yearning to love and to be loved, and I was actually quite fond of her.

of events to do more than silently open and close my mouth.

No, the speaker was Tamara Bello, last seen by me as I scurried from the burger bar following my toenail catastrophe.

And how did I feel about that? Well, happy, sad, embarrassed, confused. Mainly confused. One of the most surprising things about this situation was seeing Tamara and Ludmilla hanging out together – the coolest and the uncoolest girls in the school. It was like looking down at dinner time and seeing chips and custard on the same plate. It was another confirmation of the fact that in the world of Camp Fatso, the standard laws of the universe no longer held good.

'Y-y-you,' I finally managed to say, helped by the jolt as Ludmilla dumped me on the ground. 'What are you doing here?'

'As I said, having a perfectly good midnight feast.'

And indeed the ground was strewn with sweet wrappers, empty white boxes bearing the tell-tale marks of chocolate cake, empty cans of Coke, etc., etc.

'And why is your face all black?'

'Ah, well . . . it's complicated . . .' I dabbed at my face with my hankie. 'So, you've been sent to Camp Fitso . . . ?'

'Duh.'

Now, obviously, as I said before, 'Duh' is a pretty stupid thing to say, but I supposed I'd earned this one.

'But why do you need midnight feasts? Isn't it a kind of paradise here? A paradise of food and fun?'

'Ha! Funny, that's what we say about your side

of the fence. But no, it's not paradise. It's OK,
I guess, but there's only so much steamed fish
a girl can take. Anyway, what the heck are you
doing climbing over the wall?'

'Because it's a hellhole over there. They starve
us and make us dig up worms and—'

But that was as far as we got in that particular
conversation. For at that moment we were
blinded by the dazzling beam of a searchlight.

'STAY RIGHT WHERE YOU ARE,' came
a commanding voice from a megaphone. 'WE
HAVE YOU COVERED. ANY ATTEMPT TO
ESCAPE WILL BE MET WITH MAXIMUM
FORCE.'

'Pfumpf,' said Ludmilla.

Tamara used a very bad word indeed.

And then suddenly her attitude completely
changed.

'Listen very carefully – we don't have much time. We've clearly been betrayed. We're not really at Camp Fitso to get fit – we've been sent by the Badges Protection League.'

'The what?'

'I told you to shut up and listen. We were going to go under the wall into Camp Fatso. But now we'll never get another chance, so it's up to you. Hut Nineteen. Go there. Rescue the badges. Understand?

'No . . .'

Suddenly we were surrounded by goons – except that these weren't really goons, but goonettes, i.e. lady goons. Which doesn't mean that they were nice and ladylike – in fact they were horrid, shouting and pushing and jabbing at us with paintball guns. In this manner we were led to a building at the heart of Camp Fitso.

As I'd seen from the human pyramid, everything on this side of the wall was much more pleasant than on the boys' side, and the building we entered was all big windows and shining steel and polished stone floors. The goonettes took us to an office. I was made to sit on a bench outside, while the girls went in. As they passed me, Ludmilla stumbled and barged into Tamara, who in turn crashed into me.

'Don't forget, Hut Nineteen,' she said, and I felt her cram something into the trouser pocket of my orange tracksuit. I didn't immediately check to see what it was in case it attracted attention.

I sat outside the office for ten minutes, sandwiched between two goonettes. I tried to make conversation, but the goonettes weren't the talking kind.

And then Ludmilla and Tamara came out, looking cowed. I managed to mouth, 'Get help!' at Tamara. Unfortunately, mouthing reasonably complicated things never works very well. She might easily have thought I said, 'Sausage, marshmallow, banana, Humpty Dumpty,' although I admit that would have been a really stupid thing to say right then. Or at any other time.

The office was huge. There was a figure sitting in a swivel chair, facing away from me, its occupant surveying Camp Fitso through the big window. Slowly the chair spun to face me. Bizarrely, the arms of the chair were formed from two stuffed badgers. But that wasn't what shocked me. What shocked me was the person in the chair. Shocking and horrifying, and yet also inevitable.

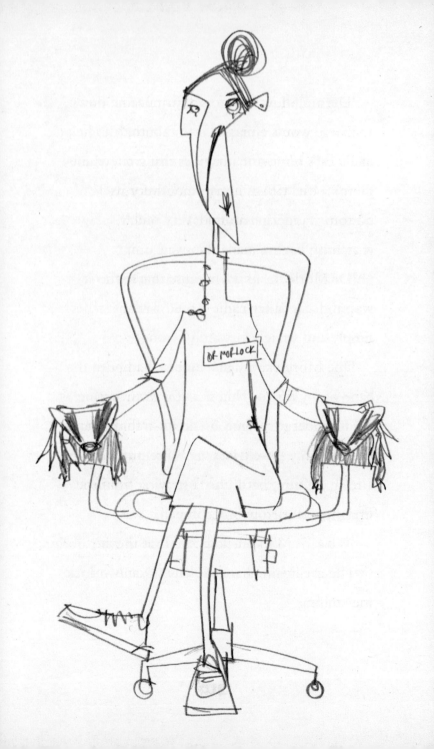

'Dermot, how nice to see you. Do sit down.'

These words emerged from a mouth so like a cat's bum, one imagines that somewhere there's a cat with a human mouth for its bottom wandering around, very much regretting having made the swap.

'Dr Morlock,' I said, because that's who it was, and any other name would have been simply and straightforwardly wrong.

Doc Morlock, my nutritionist, had been the bane of my life for almost a year now, forcing me to undergo a rigorous, donut-free diet, and checking my – well, let's say waste products – to make sure that I wasn't straying from the straight and narrow broccoli path.

'What . . . ? I mean, how . . . ? I mean who . . . ?'

The cat's bum changed shape. Doc Morlock was smiling.

'You didn't know that I was the
Oberkommandant of Camps Fatso and Fitso?'

'No . . . I just thought you were . . .'

'A simple nutritionist? Oh, no, let me tell
you that I have greater ambitions than that.
I plan to roll out Camp Fatsos all over the
country, improving the health and vitality of
the nation's young people.'

'And making tons of money for yourself,'
I said. Or rather, thought, as I'm basically a
coward.

'However, we're here to talk about *you*,
Dermot. I feel rather let down by you. Trying
to escape in that frankly amateurish way. Did
you really think you could do it?'

'I—'

'But the more important question is what to
do with you now? I could, of course, just have

you thrown in the cooler for a couple of days. That should help you to see reason. Or, if I felt that this sort of insubordination was going to continue, then I could see about extending your stay with us well beyond the end of next week.'

'But you can't! My mum—'

'Would be delighted if I were to keep you on here, in a permanent residential capacity. Especially if I were to offer her a reduced rate. As you've seen, we have excellent educational and recreational facilities. And you know that your mother has absolute faith in my judgement.'

That bit was true. They did yoga together, and my mum used to speak in awe of Doc Morlock's ability to hold in her wind, which is apparently a big thing in yoga circles. I didn't know if the threat had real teeth, or just a mouthful of gums.

But I didn't want to take the chance. I couldn't stand it much longer in this place.

'I'll be good,' I said. And I think I may have meant it. 'I beg you, just the cooler—'

'We'll see, Dermot, we'll see. And for your sake, I hope you're telling the truth. And by the way, we know exactly who helped you to get over the fence. You'll be pleased, I'm sure, to find out that you'll all be sharing the same reward for this.'

'But,' I said, thinking aloud, 'what's to stop me telling everyone about this place when I get back? They'll close you down. Worse, they'll—'

'Love me for it. Imagine the headlines. "Blimp complains of harsh regime in fat camp." And then they'll see the before and after photographs. Parents will beg me to take their loathsome couch potatoes. This country is suffering from an epidemic of obesity, in case you hadn't realized. OK, you've taken up quite enough of my time.'

And then Doc Morlock rang a little bell on her desk, and two goonettes came in. I was put in the back of a van with CAMP FITSO: WHERE YOUR DREAMS OF HEALTH COME TRUE! written on the side in jaunty lettering. After a bumpy five-minute ride around the perimeter, I was released back into the hands of my own friendly goons, Badwig and, of course, Boss Skinner, both looking very annoyed at being woken up in the early hours of the morning.

Skinner came very close to me.

'I hope you like yourself, son,' he said, in that terrifyingly quiet way of his, 'because for the next few days you're all you've got.'

Then they marched me to my old cell and

kicked me inside. Badwig threw in a thin blanket.

'Make yourself comfortable,' he laughed as I squirmed on the bare floor.

And, just as Doc Morlock had said, my friends were in the other cells. I heard a noise like someone slowly strangling a goose, which could only be Igor blowing away at his mouth organ. And from somewhere, the sound of Flo's tears.

They left us rotting there for the whole of Saturday and Saturday night, and only dragged us out on Sunday evening, which is when I'm writing this. All that time in the cold and the dark, with nothing but those creepy meat carcasses for company, and the sound of the strangled goose, and Flo weeping.

In case you're wondering, there was a

bucket for a toilet. And I'm not even going to talk about how disgusting that was. You'll have to imagine it. Actually, no, don't imagine it. Think of something nice. Some flowers or butterflies, that sort of thing.

Twice a day the door opened and a goon brought in a cup of water and a carrot.

I'd have gone mad, I think, if it hadn't been for one thing. I found it in the pocket of my filthy tracksuit. It had been put there by Tamara as she stumbled into me.

It was a donut.

She had given me the gift of a donut.

Sometimes a donut can be more than just a donut.

It can be a symbol.

And sometimes it's just a donut.

Was this a symbol donut, or a donut donut?

More confusion.

As a little kid, when there was nothing on the telly I used to sit and watch our washing machine. I was kind of fascinated by the way the clothes and suds all churned around. Well, that's what the inside of my head was like now. Spinning and churning. But not getting the clothes clean, of course.

If it was a symbol donut, I should probably keep it, because those kinds of donuts don't come along very often. But then I was very hungry. And so, of course, were my friends.

And that's when I decided to break it up and share it out, tossing the chunks along to the others through the bars. So it did become a symbol donut. A symbol of our friendship and our solidarity against the cruelties of Camp Fatso.

I ate my fragment crumb by crumb, like Charlie eating the Wonka bar he gets for his birthday.

So, at last I have a donut count:

DONUT COUNT:

Monday 9 April

This morning, before breakfast, we had a secret
Hut Four talk. The subject, of course, was
betrayal. As Doc Morlock had told me, someone
had snitched our plan.

'It had to be Gogol,' said Igor.

I agreed.

'Are we sure it was anyone?' said J-Man.
'Couldn't it just have been that the goons
eyeballed you? Or maybe those two chicks got
seen, and we all got caught as collateral damage?'

'Just a quick tip, J-Man,' I said. 'In case you ever meet them, don't call Tamara or Ludmilla a "chick" to their faces or you'll be like the guy who asked for crushed nuts with his ice cream and ended up in hospital. But the truth is, if someone looks like a traitor, acts like a traitor and happens to be the only one of us who didn't get thrown in the cooler, then logic says that he must be the traitor. The only question is what we do about it.'

'Hello, old chap, delighted to make your acquaintance,' said Dong.

'I hear you, China D,' said J-Man, shaking his head sadly, 'but that's a tough thing to do, even to a snitch.'

'What?' I had no idea what he was talking about.

'The Oriental Deester was saying that we

should use the traditional snitch's punishment on Gogol. Ain't that right, Dong?'

The Chinese kid smiled politely. 'Hello, old chap, delighted to make your acquaintance.'

J-Man nodded, as if resigned to the inevitable.

'What is the traditional punishment?' I asked.

He told me.

'Let's take a vote,' he said, looking deadly serious, as well he might.

He went round the room, asking each of us in turn.

'Donut?'

'I say yes.'

'Dong?'

'Hello, old chap, delighted to make your acquaintance.'

'OK, that's another yes.'

'Igor?'

Igor silently shook his head.

'Fair enough, big guy. You got a kind heart.'

'Flo?'

Florian had his hands cupped around a
ladybird he had found.

'Didn't like it in the nasty cooler, did we,
Lady? Ernesto should be sorry for what he did,
but he hasn't said sorry, has he? And if you don't
say sorry then you've got to be punished.'

In the afternoon Mr Fricker looked strangely
pleased to see me.

'Good to have you back with us,' he said,
although he couldn't stop his hands from making
the by now traditional strangling motions.

Luckily we'd moved on from Peruvian
shoe-throwing.

'Today's World Sport,' Fricker announced, 'is

Eskimo seal-wrestling. Right, I need a volunteer to be the seal . . . You, Dermot? Good man.'

I don't really want to say much about what followed, except that I was stripped down to my boxer shorts, covered in grease and . . . Well, you can fill in the rest for yourselves.

In the evening I ate my gruel and even considered eating the piece of meat. But the image of the things hanging in the cooler haunted me, and I just couldn't make myself do it, even though my poor body was crying out for sustenance. There was another reason I couldn't eat much: I knew what was coming. And that was enough to kill even a raging appetite.

At midnight the hut began to stir. J-Man shook me awake – I'd fallen asleep and was in the middle of a dream about – well, you can guess.

We gathered around Gogol's bunk. J-Man shone the beam of his torch in the creepy kid's face. He woke with a startled cry.

'Hey! What's—'

But he never had the chance to say anything more. Igor put his hand over his mouth.

'You have been found guilty of the offence of being a snitch,' J-Man intoned in his deep voice. 'And the penalty for snitching is—'

Gogol seemed to know what was coming and he began to fight. But Igor and Dong easily subdued him. Flo attached a device to his feet – a chain made from tin cans strung together with shoelaces.

'Get him to the door,' said J-Man.

Gogol was now begging. 'You can't do this. I'm innocent. I didn't snitch on nobody.' His eyes were wide, and his zits were popping.

'Do we really have to do this?' I said to J-Man.

'Too late to go back now, boy,' he said. 'In any case, we gotta send out a message. You mess with the boys of Hut Four, you get messed up right back.'

I opened the door. Gogol was still fighting like a demon. He clutched at the door frame, but I prised his grip loose. Igor and J-Man were too strong. Together they hurled him out into the darkness. Gogol landed with a *thunk* and a *clank* from the cans. He tried to move, and the cans rattled and clanked louder. Suddenly the night was lit up with the piercing beam of a searchlight. We all ran to the windows. The beam had found Gogol. He tried to run from it, but there was nowhere to hide.

'No!' he screamed. 'I'm not escaping – it's a mistake – it's—'

But then his voice was cut off by the deafening rattle from a high-power automatic paintball cannon, unleashing ten 20mm paintballs a second. The red shells crashed into Gogol. He reeled and staggered, like a puppet controlled by a drunken puppeteer. He fell, and still the red horror rained down on him. With one last, supernatural effort he dragged himself up and ran towards another of the huts, but the machine guns cut him down again.

Sickened, I turned away and so I missed the final act. But I heard the shouts of the goons, heard the yapping of the sausage dogs, heard, above all else, the utter silence from the splattered body of Ernesto Gogol.

Dong looked at me. 'Hello, old chap, delighted to make your acquaintance,' he said, in a way that was sad, guilty and accusatory all at the same time.

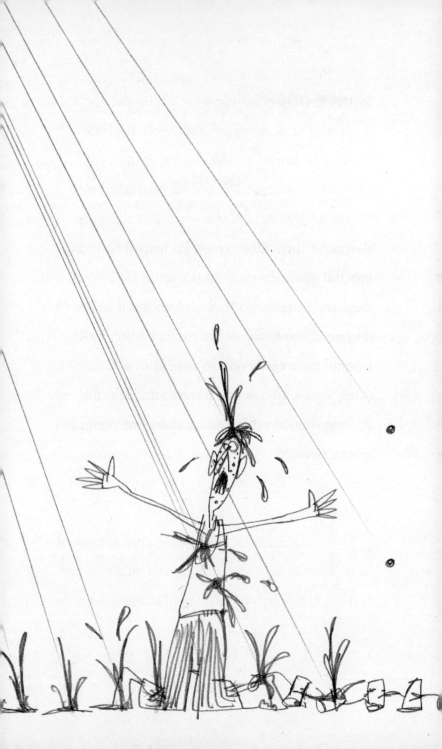

DONUT COUNT:

NO
donuts

Zero, of course. But even if I'd had a brimming
box full of the finest donuts ever made by
the hand of man, I'd have said no thanks, so
disgusted was I with what we had done. Well,
I might have eaten one or two, in case it gave
offence to whoever had gone to the effort of
making them. Perhaps just a chocolate icing, and
a butterscotch.

Tuesday 10 April

We never saw Ernesto Gogol again. Either he was sent to another camp, or perhaps – and I hope this is true – he was released on compassionate grounds. He'd done his dirty work for the goons, and been punished for it. Now I hoped he could find some peace and forgiveness.

Anyway, on the next day's worm hunt I mentioned the mysterious Hut Nineteen to J-Man.

He hesitated for a moment, then shook his head.

'Ain't no such hut. Ain't never spoken to no boy from Hut Nineteen. No sir.'

'But what about these badges that Tamara mentioned? Do you know what they could be?'

'Badges? Well, we all got these.' He pointed at the insignia on the left breast of the tracksuit – three boys, one fat, one just overweight, one skinny. 'Guess she talkin' 'bout that.'

And then a paintball shell thumped into the ground right between us, spraying us in a gory red mist.

'You boys want to find out what it feels like to get one of these babies in the face?' asked Boss Skinner, his quiet voice somehow carrying the twenty metres from his truck to our worm hole.

'No, Boss,' I said, and got digging.

★ ★ ★

I arrived back at the hut tired and dirty and
depressed, but something, or rather someone, was
waiting for me there who put an astounded grin
on my face.

'RENFREW! What on earth . . . ? Is it just
you, or are the other guys here?' I babbled.

Renfrew smiled his little rodenty smile. It was

the best thing I'd seen since the beginning of my Camp Fatso ordeal.

'It's just me – Spam and Corky are still away on holiday. I got a text from Tamara Bello. She said she'd had to bribe one of the guards to get her phone back, and that you were in desperate trouble and I had to get in here to help you.'

Renfrew always made a strange sort of 'ungth' sound before he spoke. It could be quite annoying at times, but now it was music to my ears.

'Trouble's right. Did you tell my mum and dad what was going on?'

'I tried. I said Camp Fatso was rubbish and like a jail, but your mum said that it was just you kicking up a fuss about not having any donuts for a couple of weeks. She said that your nutritionist warned her that you'd be like this, but that in the end you'd be happier and healthier.'

'What did my dad say?'

'I didn't see him. Er . . . he was in the—'

'Don't tell me, the toilet.' Did I mention
that my dad hides from life in the toilet all day?
Well, he does. 'But how the heck did you get
in here?'

'That part was easy. I told my parents that I
actually wanted to go to Camp Fatso, and they
jumped at it. My dad's always been worried that
I'm too much of a weakling, and they think
I'll get some muscles and learn to stick up for
myself. And it was dead cheap, because the Camp
Fatso people said that some kid had just had to
leave early . . .'

'Ah, yes, that would be Ernesto. You're sitting
on his bed.'

At that moment I sensed the others come into
the hut and fan out behind me.

'Is this a new boy I see before me?' said
J-Man.

'You won't believe this, but he's a friend of
mine,' I said. 'From the outside.'

'Hmph,' said J-Man, unimpressed. 'That don't
change nothin'. You know what we gotta do to a
new boy.'

He sounded tough, but he gave me a little
wink.

'What's he talking about, Donut?' Renfrew
asked, looking a little worried. In fact, as he saw
my massive hut buddies looming around him, he
looked *very* worried.

'Sorry, old friend,' I replied ruefully. 'But
tradition is important here. PILE ON!!!!!'

We didn't give Renfrew the full treatment – it
would have squashed him flat. It was just enough
to make him feel like one of us.

Afterwards I did the introductions, and then we told Renfrew what had been going on here. He shook his head in amazement.

'I wouldn't believe you if it wasn't for the stuff I dug up on the internet. It's mostly rumours, but there are some amazing things about the history of the place.'

'Like what?'

'Like in the Second World War it was a prison camp for captured Italians.'

'No way!'

'It totally was, and there was a bust out in 1944. They dug a tunnel and . . .'

His tale ran on excitedly and only stopped with the siren announcing PE, at which point it was my turn to astonish Renfrew by telling him the identity of the new Camp Fatso PE instructor.

That afternoon's World Sport was angry Japanese
grunting (the angriest grunter is the winner, and
you get disqualified if you accidentally miaow or
make any other cat noises). As this involved very
few opportunities to make my life miserable,
Mr Fricker followed it up with a quick round
of Smack the Rhino, a game originating in
Mozambique.

And yes, I was, surprise surprise, the rhino.

Fricker hardly batted an eyelid when he
saw Renfrew, which I thought was a bit odd. I
suppose Renfrew isn't quite as noticeable as me,
being small and gerbil-like. But still, as I say, it
was strange . . .

At dinner time we had a long, droning talk from

Badwig about ingratitude, and how some people were determined to spoil it for all the others, which was why the carrot ration was being further reduced.

'I name no names,' he said, looking straight at our table, 'but you can all work out who is responsible for this and take appropriate action.' Then he pointed at us in case anyone hadn't got it yet. Using the age-old tactic of divide and rule, it neatly turned the anger away from the goons and onto us. So while trudging back to Hut Four we had to endure punches and kicks and general, all-purpose abuse from the rest of the camp.

But for once I didn't really care. I didn't care, because I had a plan. OK, not really a plan. More just a thing to do. But having a thing to do is the best thing short of an actual plan for slightly cheering you up. Especially when you've got an old friend to do it with.

DONUT COUNT:

So far, anyway. But I suppose there's always the faint chance that I might stumble across one on my way to Hut Nineteen.

Wednesday 11 April

Horror!

Horror!

Horror!

And in case I haven't got my point across adequately,

HORROR!

I slipped from my bed at midnight and woke Renfrew. We were quiet, but not quiet enough.

'Where you guys going?'

It was J-Man, as ever watching over us.

'I'm showing Renfrew the way to the latrine hut.'

I'd decided to keep my plan secret from the rest of the hut. It wasn't that I didn't trust them, it was just that I thought the fewer people in the know, the smaller the chance of something leaking out. Plus, if we were caught, the others wouldn't have to face the cooler again, which was something I really didn't want to have on my conscience.

'Cain't he use the bucket like everybody else?' groaned J-Man.

'Hey, he's only little – if he falls in he'll drown.'

'If the goons catch you, you goin' in the cooler again. Maybe this time you don't come out.'

'We'll take our chances. Can I borrow your torch?'

'Take it. But you turn that sucker on and the goons will be all over you like flies on a cow flop.'

'I hear you. It's for when we're in the latrine. We'll be careful.'

'Mind you are. I don't wanna lose that flashlight.'

Luckily there was just enough light from the half-moon for us to see without the torch.

'You sure you know where you're going?' I hissed to Renfrew.

'Of course. I printed the plan out from the internet.' He pointed to a piece of crumpled paper – I really didn't want to know where he'd hidden it when he sneaked it into the camp. 'See, this line is the fence, and we just follow it round

to here, where there's an opening indicated. That
leads to Hut Nineteen.'

I thought again about what Renfrew had
told me.

'It was all there on the internet,' he said.
'Most of it was in Italian, but I just ran it through

an online translation engine. What we call Hut Nineteen, they called *Capanna Diciannove*.'

'What does that mean?'

'Hut Nineteen, doofus, but in Italian.'

'Oh, OK. But how do you know that their Hut Nineteen is the same as our Hut Nineteen? I mean, surely Camp Fatso isn't just using the same huts today as back in the war?'

Renfrew nodded. 'After the war the camp became a British Army training camp. Then the army sold it and the huts were used for battery chickens. Then the Camp Fatso people bought it. I've checked the plans for the old camp against the satellite images of the present camp, and it's a perfect match. These are exactly the same huts, on the same foundations.'

The searchlight swept over the field at 12.15 a.m., but I'd anticipated it and dragged

Renfrew down onto the ground. The dogs
would be harder to avoid, but I planned to cross
that sausage dog when I came to it.

In a few minutes we came to the gap in
the fence marked on Renfrew's map. There
was a sign:

What did that mean? Minefield? No, that
would be against the Geneva Convention,
surely? It must have just been an empty warning.

The gap in the fence was actually more of a
corridor, or a tunnel, as the wire continued on

each side. I was about to lead the way through when Renfrew put his hand on my arm. He pointed to a leaf floating down from one of the trees just outside the fence. For a second it was caught in a red beam.

'Motion sensor lasers,' said Renfrew, 'set into the fence post.'

For a second I imagined a laser cutting me completely in half, and my poor chubby legs running around for a while before they realized what had happened, and fell over.

'I thought this was all a bit too easy,' I said.

I also wondered what could be so important about Hut Nineteen that it needed this sort of security. My half-starved brain thought for a second or two that perhaps this was where they kept the donuts, and I felt my mouth fill with drool. But no, whatever lay at the heart of this mystery, it was unlikely to be a ring of deep-fried dough, dusted with icing sugar, still warm . . .

Focus. I had to focus.

I had no idea how many lasers there were, cutting across the corridor. There was a faint chance that there might just be this first one, but the evidence of almost every computer game I'd ever played suggested that there would be loads of them, zigzagging across the path like a cat's cradle. The first beam – the only one I had seen – was perhaps half a metre up from the ground. Too high for most fat kids to jump, and too low for them to crawl under, without a fat butt-cheek cutting the beam and either setting off the alarm (most likely) or getting sliced off by the high-powered laser (less likely, as this wasn't a game, but real life).

Too low for most fat kids, but . . . I still hadn't

eaten any of the weird meat they'd been serving up, so I'd been 'living' on a diet of gruel and carrots for over a week now. I felt at the waistband of my tracksuit. It was loose. I'd lost an awful lot of puppy fat since I'd been here. Could I, perhaps, fit under the beam?

'OK, Renfrew,' I said. 'Let's do this.'

I threw myself down, and began to crawl and squirm on my belly. Crawling on your belly is one of those things that looks fairly easy, and is in fact fairly easy for the first couple of metres. It then goes from being uncomfortable, to very, very uncomfortable, to utterly, agonizingly hard. Plus, there was that whole getting-my-bum-lasered-off thing, which I knew probably wouldn't happen. But then eleven days ago I'd have said that everything that's happened to me over the past ten days could never happen, so you never know. And if there really were laser beams, could I rule out landmines? Maybe left over from the war when Camp Fatso was a prison camp? I wondered, as I crawled, if it would be better to be blown sky-high by a landmine or have one of my buttocks sliced off by the laser. True, with the landmine, I'd be pretty much 100 per cent dead, which was a very poor outcome by anyone's reckoning. But having a buttock sliced off would be pretty embarrassing too. How would I ride a bike? You need the full set of buttocks for that, or you'd just slide off, to general ridicule.

Well, either there weren't any lasers or we successfully scrunched beneath them, for we came through the tunnel with all our buttocks intact.

'You OK?' I asked Renfrew as we brushed the grass and leaves off our clothes.

'Fine. Rather enjoying all this, actually.'

I could sort of see how this might be fun for Renfrew. His parents thought that playing the violin and doing maths puzzles counted as entertainment, so crawling through the mud on your belly after a day of eating gruel and making Japanese grunting sounds was probably quite enjoyable.

Renfrew checked his map again and pointed. 'It should be just beyond those trees.'

We followed a little path through the screen of scrubby trees, and there, looming up before us in the moonlight, was Hut Nineteen. And now I didn't have to concentrate on not being lasered, I noticed something else: the smell. It was deep and rich and truly terrible, like a lasagne made from a tramp's underpants and dog sick.

I couldn't see anyone around, although I did hear the distant yapping of a sausage dog.

I hurried to the hut, through the growing stench. Four wooden steps led up to the door. I tugged at the handle.

'Locked!'

Maybe we should have taken that as our cue to get the heck out of there. But now we had come this far, we had to go on.

'There's a window,' said Renfrew.

It was shut, but the wood was ancient and rotten, and a shove with the palm of my hand forced it open.

'Up you go,' I said to Renfrew.

'Why me?'

'Because I'm in charge of this mission, plus that window frame looks a bit rotten, and it might break if I step on it.'

I also suspected that even in my new, slightly thinner form, I was still too fat to squeeze

through the window. Renfrew, on the other
hand, could have been made for squeezing

through small spaces. I gave him a boost up.

'When you're in you can open the door for me from the inside.'

He stuck his head through the window, then drew it back, like someone snatching their hand from a flame.

'Reeks,' he said. 'And there's something alive in there. I can hear it . . .'

'Just get on with it, Renfrew,' I said rather sternly, and gave him a helpful shove. He half fell through, then scurried round to the door. He opened it, and a wave of stench flowed out, carrying Renfrew with it. His face was tight with terror.

'I'm not going back in,' he said, trembling. 'It's . . . it's horrible.'

'OK,' I sighed. 'You wait here then. You can be the lookout.'

I took J-Man's torch from my pocket, held my breath and walked into Hut Nineteen.

It was like walking into hell itself, such was the stench. It clung to me, thick as Marmite. There was a noise. A restless noise. A shuffling. And perhaps, somewhere, a hiss. Or a sigh. I sensed that the hut was full, but full of what?

I flicked the torch on, and still I could not understand what its beam revealed. Boxes. No, not boxes. Cages. Small cages, stacked from the floor almost to the ceiling, filling every available space.

I moved closer to one of the stacks, trembling. I shone the light through the chicken wire. And there, cowering in the corner of the cage, I saw, not a badge, but . . .

'A badger?' J-Man's eyes were wide with

disbelief. 'You are one crazy dude. Ain't no badgers in cages. Why'd anyone want to do a damn fool thing like that?'

It was the next morning, i.e. today. We were trudging through the woods on our way to dig worms.

'Yes – you see, Tamara didn't say "badges" but "badgers". I figured it all out. The meat. The stuff they give you with the gruel. It's badger. Has to be. And those carcasses hanging in the cooler? Badger for sure. And you know what was in their feeding trays? Worms. Yeah, worms. That's why we spend our days out in these woods, digging. We're all part of this.'

'Boy, have you been reading books again, or what? Nobody eat badger. Nobody keep badgers in cages. I say you fell asleep in the john and dreamed it all up.'

'Both of us?' said Renfrew.

'Yeah, well, you're a new kid, and what new kids say don't count.'

'I know what I saw, J-Man. And I know it's not right. And I want to break them loose.'

'And how you gonna do that, even if you *is* right? You couldn't even get your own self out of here. You think you can stroll out through them gates with two hundred badgers down your pants? You got a bit more room down there than when you first came here, but not enough for that kind of payload.'

'There's a tunnel. Dug by the Italians in the war. Renfrew found old letters from the prisoners in an archive on the internet. Prisoners who escaped.'

'Really? And where that tunnel be?'

'Ah, well, I don't know, exactly.'

'That ain't much use, is it?'

'There must be a way of finding it. Somehow we've got to get those badgers out of there. And we have to do it by Friday. There was a schedule pinned to the inside of the door of Hut Nineteen. Feeding times, that sort of thing. And then, for Friday evening, there was a black cross. It means that's when they're going to kill them. I know it. And you've got to help me.'

J-Man did his now familiar slow head–shake, and then he started breaking up the ground with his pick. After a while he said to me, 'Lardies might know if there's a tunnel. If you want I can fix for you to see the boy Hercule Paine. I don't recommend it, no sir. But if that's what you want, then be it on your own head.'

'You can do that?' I said, my hopes putting in a little spurt. 'I thought he hated you, and you hated him?'

'That about the size of it. But I still got some influence. I ain't happy about it, but I see what I can do. This gonna cost you. This gonna cost me. You make a pact with the devil, the only coin he care about is your soul.'

And then J-Man hit the turf with his pick so hard I thought he was going to open up a crack to the molten core of the earth itself.

The message came back through J-Man, though he couldn't even bear to look me in the eye as he told me.

'You get yourself to Hut One after dinner.'

The other guys heard what he said.

'You shouldn't go there,' rumbled Igor. 'Only trouble will come. You should stay and play chess with me.'

'Yeah,' said Flo. 'You shouldn't see the bad boys. The bad boys are bad. You should stay with the goodies.'

'Hello, old chap, delighted to make your acquaintance,' said Dong, but he got his message across pretty well too.

'Sorry, guys. I've got to do this.'

'Why?' said Igor. 'I don't understand. Why are you going to see the Lardies? Are you joining them?'

'Nah, nothing like that. I can't tell you any more. It might get you into trouble. Let's just say that it's something I have to do. You've just got to look after Renfrew for me while I'm gone.'

'Sure thing.'

I didn't really need to ask. Renfrew had become a sort of pet to the Hut Four guys.

And so it was that I found myself knocking on the door of Hut One after dinner this evening.

The door opened, and there in front of me was the one they called Demetrius the Destroyer. He had a face like a half-eaten pork pie. The word was that he'd once bitten the head off one of the sausage dogs for making the mistake of yapping at him. I didn't know if that was really true, but I wasn't going to put it to the test by yapping.

'Boss, the Donut kid's here,' he said out of the side of his mouth, without taking his eyes off me.

'Spread 'em,' he said.

'What?'

'Against the wall. I gotta frisk you.'

So I put my hands against the wall and let the big lummox pat me down. He did it with all the

gentleness of someone trying to beat a monkey
to death.

From the outside, the hut had been
indistinguishable from all the others. The inside
was a different story. In place of the hard wooden
floor and hard wooden chairs and hard wooden

beds, there were the softest of soft furnishings: a
carpet thick enough to swallow a midget, easy
chairs draped in rich fabrics, and a four-poster

bed, like something Henry VIII would have considered a bit too showy. I didn't see anywhere for the other Lardies to sleep, and supposed that they must be the residents of Hut Two.

But they were here in strength now. As well as the mountainous Demetrius the Destroyer, I saw Gilbert Pasternak with his LOVE and HAET tattoos, plus a couple of other bruisers, looking like barrage balloons painted with angry faces. And there, on a long couch, propped up by satin cushions like a bloated slug, lay Hercule Paine himself. He was eating grapes.

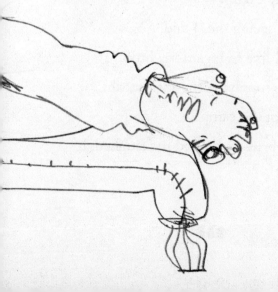

'Dear, dear boy,' he said. 'Do come in and make yourself at home. I apologize for the security precautions. I trust that Demetrius wasn't too . . . rough? He has a gentle soul, but on occasion he can be somewhat over-exuberant.'

I thought about the sausage dog he was reputed to have bitten in half. Maybe he was just playing with it . . .

I sat down on a chair. It was the softest thing my bum had touched since I'd left home. It was probably the softest thing it had ever touched, except for the time I accidentally sat on my sister Ruby's birthday cake.

'Thanks for seeing me,' I said.

'Not at all. I like to regard my little organization as supplying the various, ah, welfare needs of the camp.'

One of the bruisers behind me laughed. It

sounded like a knife blade being sharpened.

'So, how can I be of assistance?'

'I need to get out of here. And I need to take some, er, things with me.'

'A common desire. But a futile one. And your time at Camp Fatso is almost up. Why not quietly see out your time and go back home a thinner, happier boy?'

Another chuckle from behind me.

I thought about the schedule. About the terrified eyes. About the meat.

'I need to get out before Friday.'

'I know I said that I could help – but I cannot work miracles. I—'

'I know that there's a tunnel. An escape tunnel. Dug by the Italians.'

'A tunnel? Italians? What an imagination you have.'

But I knew I was right. A flickering eyelid told me so. As did the sudden silence in the rest of the room.

I stared into his piggy black eyes.

'Where is it, Hercule?'

I felt a stinging slap on the back of my head.

'Mr Paine to you.'

'No, no, Gilbert, there's no need for violence. Yet. Let us suppose that there *was* such a tunnel. Why should I tell you about it? What is there in it for me?'

'Does there have to be something in it for you? Couldn't you just tell me because it's the right thing to do?'

Hercule Paine smiled. He had the kind of mouth that becomes slightly smaller when it smiles. It was almost indistinguishable from a look of disgust.

'The right thing to do. What a quaint notion. Haven't you realized yet where you are, my dear Donut? Look around you. How much goodness and virtue do you see here?'

'I—'

'You see people acting according to the dictates of power. To have power is to have right on your side. Morality is the slave of the boys with the strongest arms. And that's me, Donut. What you see here is the truth, undisguised, unadorned. It's why I love it.'

'You're a monster, Paine.' SLAP. It didn't stop me. 'But there are boys here who don't think like you. Kids who still value truth and honour and decency. Kids like—'

'J-Man?' Now Paine's smile grew, becoming a grin, showing his teeth, which seemed unnaturally small and weak, as if his adult teeth had never come through. And as Paine grinned, the others guffawed. 'Oh, how very, very amusing. You don't know, do you? I'd assumed that you would have worked it out by now.'

'What are you talking about?' But even as I spoke the words, I knew. 'J-Man—'

'Is my creature. Of course he is.'

'And it was him who told the goons about the first escape bid?'

Hercule Paine inclined his head, as if accepting a compliment.

'And Ernesto . . . ?'

'A necessary sacrifice.'

I felt sick. Sick and angry. J-Man was a Lardy. Or a spy for the Lardies. A fink. A fake. A phoney.

'But perhaps there is an arrangement we can come to. I have a certain interest in maintaining the status quo around here – it's why I prefer for there not to be too many escapes or other disruptions. However, I could make an exception.'

'What do you mean?'

'Well, it so happens that you are correct. There *is* an old escape tunnel. It begins under one of the huts, and carries on for a couple of hundred metres, out beyond the perimeter fence and into the woods.'

'Which hut?'

'Well, it's here that we engage in a touch of mutual back-scratching. You see, for that information, you must help me with a little problem of my own. Now, do have a grape.'

This was it. As I'd been warned, to get something from the Lardies, you had to give something, and I was about to pay.

DONUT COUNT:

NO
donuts

Of course. But even if I'd had one, I doubt I
could have eaten it, so sick did I feel about
J-Man's betrayal. Well, OK, I probably could have
eaten it. But I wouldn't have enjoyed it. Oh,
who am I kidding? If I'd been offered a donut
I would have wolfed it down and begged for
more.

Thursday 12 April

J-Man knew that something was up.

I'd avoided him all morning.

'They tell you what you need to know?' he asked, wielding his pick.

'Yep.'

The pick cut into the ground.

'There's a kind of truth that sits cheek by jowl with a lie, Donut,' he said.

'And there's a kind of liar who sits cheek by jowl with the Lardies,' I spat back.

The pick slammed into the earth a couple of centimetres from my fingers.

And then something happened to me that had never happened before. I totally lost it. I'd managed to get through twelve years without having a fight (apart from with my sisters, which always ended in tears – my tears, usually), and I didn't really know how to do it. But I threw myself at J-Man, and the surprise was enough to unbalance him. I landed on top of him and managed to stay there, shoving my knees into his chest.

I heard Renfrew shout out, 'No, Dermot, he's not worth it,' but just ignored him.

'You betrayed me. You betrayed us all,' I yelled, and tried to land a punch in his face. He got a hand up and parried it. Then he caught my wrist.

By this time the whole work party had downed

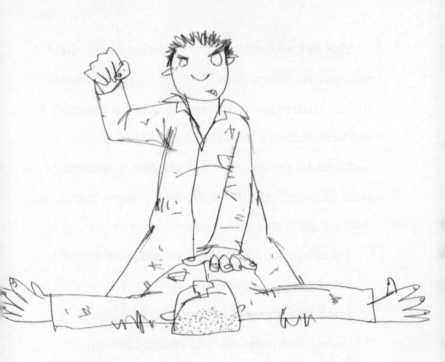

tools and gathered round. I knew the goons would
be right behind them, but I didn't care.

'Donut, you don't understand. They . . . they
made me do it. They got a . . . a hold on me.'

'I don't care. What you did to Gogol –
making him take the rap. That was unforgivable.'

The kids around us were cheering us on, the way you do when there's a fight – particularly if the alternative form of entertainment is digging for worms.

I heard a grown-up voice say, 'We stop them, Boss Skinner?' And then the answering whisper, 'No, let the girls fight it out.'

'I feel bad,' said J-Man as we struggled together. 'But I couldn't . . . I . . .'

Then he let go of my wrists and said meekly, 'Do what you gotta do,' and closed his eyes.

I drew back my fist, ready to drive it into his face.

I didn't.

I don't think I would have, even if I hadn't been shot by Boss Skinner in the back. It was the most painful thing I'd ever felt, and the force knocked me off J-Man.

'Girls done finished playing,' said Boss Skinner.

But J-Man hadn't finished. He sprang up with amazing speed for such a big kid and charged at the head goon. The boys who'd been watching dived out of the way. Of course, J-Man never reached Skinner – he was cut down by a wall of fire from the paintball guns. Four hit him in the chest, and he staggered back, but then came forward again. *Thwack, thwack, thwack.* Still he came on. And then Boss Skinner himself enacted the *coup de grâce* and sent a paintball pellet right into J-Man's forehead.

'Take these two ladies to the cooler,' he said, a smile on his thin lips.

'Can you hear me, Donut?'

It was an hour later. I was alone in the dark of

the cell. J–Man was two doors away. He'd been calling to me ever since he came round.

'Shut up, J–Man.'

'You gotta listen, Donut. It was my kid sister. They got her next door in Camp Fitso. Life good for her in there. But they told me that unless I co-operate then that all gonna change. That girl only nine years old. I had to look out for her.'

That made me think. What would I do to protect Ruby and Ella, my two nightmare sisters? OK, maybe not a good example.

'There's no excuse for what you did.'

'I know that. I see it now. I just want . . . atonement.'

'OK, you can start by telling me about Hut Nineteen.'

There was a pause. Then a heavy sigh.

'Yeah, Hut Nineteen. That where they keep the critters.'

'The badgers. I know. Why?'

'It's what makes the camp pay. They use the hair to make fancy shaving brushes for rich folk. They undercut the Chinese, and still make a big profit on account of the slave labour they got here. And they get to use up the meat. But I guess you know that.'

'And you've eaten it.'

'Once you get the taste . . . it's addictive. Especially when you ain't got nothing else but gruel. But you know what I'm saying. Is there anything you wouldn't do for a donut, Donut?'

'I wouldn't betray my friends.'

Silence.

'But you know what, Donut? You cut a deal, didn't you, with the Lardies? They gonna burn you, you know. They gonna sell you out.'

'Maybe, but I've got a plan.'

And then, in the dark and the cold, I realized that I needed J-Man for my plan to work.

'You really want redemption?' I asked.

'I want it.'

'The tunnel. You know where it is?'

'I knows.'

And he told me. And when he told me, like so many obscure truths, it turned out to be obvious.

'OK, then, J-Man,' I said. 'Listen up good, and maybe I can save you all.'

That night, once J-Man and I had been released, Renfrew and I returned to Hut Nineteen. I wanted to go alone, but Renfrew insisted on coming with me. 'If you try to get through that window, they'll find you half in and half out in the morning and feed you to the badgers.'

He had a point.

The stench hadn't died down. And the terror of the badgers hung almost as heavy in the air as the stink.

I found the loose plank exactly where J-Man had said I would. I lifted it, and the others around it. Underneath there was a trap door. I pulled it up and saw the first rungs of a roughly hewn ladder, leading down into the darkest place in the universe. But J-Man's torch made the darkness flee.

'You want to go first?' I asked Renfrew. I didn't say it, obviously, but I was thinking how the rodent thing he had going on probably made him highly adept at scurrying down holes in the ground. Plus, I balance out my fear of heights with a fear of holes.

'I think it's a job for the mission leader,' he replied, appealing to my sense of responsibility, curse him.

The ladder went down about two metres. At the bottom, a space the size of a small room had been excavated. And then the tunnel itself began. I shone the torch down it. It was dead straight, and was lined with wooden planks.

'Nice job,' I said admiringly.

'That's the Italians for you,' said Renfrew, who'd followed me down once it was clear there weren't any monsters down here. 'Rubbish at fighting, but they make a very nice escape tunnel.'

The tunnel may have been beautifully made, but it was very narrow. Could I fit in there? I shone the torch along it. Only one way to find out.

'Away you go, Renfrew,' I ordered.

'But—'

'No buts. I went first into the hole, your turn to be first along the tunnel.'

I gave Renfrew the torch, and he began to crawl. I waited till he was a couple of metres along – so I didn't have to crawl with his bum in my face – and then I followed. It was hard work. My back scraped on the ceiling, and my butt brushed the sides, but I could squeeze through. A week ago I'd have got stuck for sure. I suppose those Italians must have been quite slim.

It took us twenty minutes to squirm our way to the end of the tunnel. Renfrew, who was, as I suspected, a pretty good crawler, was waiting for me at the foot of another ladder.

'I think I should probably go first again,' I

said. Renfrew reluctantly handed me the torch, and I started to climb.

Tragically, the third run on the ladder had decayed with age and snapped. Renfrew helped break my fall, but I think I might have emitted a high-pitched, slightly girly scream, which was totally out of place in the context of World War Two escape tunnels. It also meant that Renfrew had to kneel down so I could stand on his back to reach the fourth rung. It was all pretty messy and confusing in the confined space.

'I'm glad we're not having to do this with an enemy attacking from the rear,' I said.

The exit section was even narrower than the rest of the tunnel. But I was just thin enough to press on. At the top of the ladder was another trap door. I knew that there were patrols in the woods, so I flicked off the torch, inched up

the trap door, and peered out.

It took my eyes a few moments to get used to the darkness, but then I saw that I was indeed in the woods, a hundred metres outside Camp Fatso. I listened carefully, and heard the sound of a car driving along a road in the distance. The sound of freedom.

I had an almost uncontrollable urge to fling back the trap door and run headlong towards the road. Two things stopped me. The first was the sound of yapping. If the goons on patrol in the woods caught me now, the whole plan was finished. And the second was the knowledge that I had to save the badgers, and that meant waiting until tomorrow.

So I gently lowered the door and together Renfrew and I scooted back down the tunnel, and returned, eventually, to Hut Four.

We had reconnoitred the route. Everything was now in place.

DONUT COUNT:

But just wait till tomorrow.

Friday 13 April

No work for me today. Today I prepared for the battle of a lifetime.

I've kept the mystery a secret long enough. Here's what the loathsome Hercule Paine proposed, back in the stifling warmth of Hut One.

'Friday is, as you know, the last day of the school holidays, and so, for most of the Camp Fatso inmates – those not blessed, as I am, with the gift of permanent residence – the end of their time here. This event is traditionally marked by a celebration, enjoyed by the members of staff who have laboured so hard to care for us all. And the invitation is extended to others who have helped Camp Fatso. Local dignitaries, the occasional cabinet minister, junior members of the Royal Family, the rich and the powerful: our particular brand of entertainment has drawn them all.

'We Lardies like to help out with this, as our way of saying thank you. And generally, gambling – just a little flutter, you understand – plays a major role. This . . . entertainment will take place in two parts. Firstly, a contest between two champions—'

'A contest?'

'Yes, a Clash of the Titans. You will be one of the contestants. But I think it is a contest that you will enjoy.'

'What do I have to do?'

'Eat, dear boy, eat!'

'What, gruel?'

'Oh no, not at all. The contest will be to see who can eat the greatest number of . . . donuts.'

At the mention of donuts I sort of blanked out. The world became hazy and unfocused, and my mouth filled with drool. Was he really saying that I was going to take part in a donut-eating contest? I felt like a kid who's waited up all night on Christmas Eve and actually seen Santa. But Paine was still talking and I had to zone back in.

'Word has gone around the camp about your own epic consumption, while in the outside world, of that particular deep-fried delicacy. And it has been noted that you have refrained from much of the food on offer at the camp.

It was therefore generally assumed that you were preparing yourself for this very challenge and that you would be unbeatable. My own donut champion here' – he gestured to Demetrius the Destroyer – 'is a fine eater, but the view of the experts is that he cannot stand up to a donut guzzler like you. So most of the betting is on you, Donut, my friend. You are the hot favourite. The odds are now seven to one. It means that even a modest investment on Demetrius would pay handsome dividends, should he win. You take my meaning, I'm sure . . .'

All I could think was DONUTS DONUTS DONUTS. But I had to concentrate.

'You want me to lose on purpose to this doofus?'

SMACK! And that one stung. But it was useful. It cleared my mind of the delicious donut fug.

'It would be a very good idea, I think, if that were to happen. Good for everyone. You will get your escape. I will make a lot of money.'

'And if I don't?'

'Then I will ensure that you rot here for the rest of your fat childhood, and your friends in Hut Four will suffer . . . reprisals.'

'And secondly?'

'I beg your pardon?'

'You said the entertainment was in two parts.'

'Ah, yes. Do you know what the dachshund was originally bred for?'

'Yapping?'

'Not at all. It was bred to pursue, subdue and kill . . . the badger.'

'What? No!'

'Oh, yes. And so after the first round of amusements . . . well, I'm sure your imagination is vivid enough to paint the picture.'

The monster smiled blandly, as if we'd been discussing the weather or the weekend football results.

So that was it. The awful truth. Or rather an even awfuller bit of the truth that I already knew was pretty awful. And yet, to get what I wanted, I was going to have to steep myself in the corruption of the Camp Fatso Lardies.

But on the plus side I was going to eat a MOUNTAIN OF DONUTS.

Anyway, back to Friday. There was to be no worm dig on this, our last full day. And I knew why: the badgers would be sacrificed tonight, so there was no need to supply more food.

What it meant was that we had a full day of

World Sports with Mr Fricker. In the morning none of us really got to grips with Maori asymmetrical tennis, a game played by teams of seven on one side and nine on the other, on a court shaped like a jellyfish, with a moveable net and a ball traditionally made from a live wallaby. The part of the net was played by me and that of the wallaby by Renfrew, who was the nearest creature to an actual wallaby the camp could manage.

Mr Fricker became increasingly irate with our inability to understand the rules, but he was rapidly losing his authority, partly because it was the end of our stay at Camp Fatso, and partly because the toothbrush attachment he'd used that morning had got stuck, and it's always quite hard to take a person seriously when they have a toothbrush for a hand.

After lunch – two carrots, as a special last-day treat – we had an intense session of Norwegian ear-flicking, a game apparently invented by the Vikings to help pass the time in between raids.

And then, to cap off our sporting journey around the globe, Mr Fricker announced that we were to play a final round of British Bulldog.

Given all the beatings (and flickings) I'd taken in the previous sports, my heart sank. If you've never played British Bulldog (and you probably never should), one person is the bulldog and stands in the middle of the field. Everyone else has to run past him (or her, if it's a lady bulldog) and reach the other end. The bulldog tries to grab the runners long enough to shout, 'British Bulldog, one, two, three!' The person so caught becomes a bulldog, and they then work together to catch more people, converting them into bulldogs.

All sounds like a perfectly normal game of tag, except that the aim is to cause as much physical damage to the enemy as possible, whether you're catching or running. The most dangerous position is that of the first bulldog. There's a real chance of just basically getting trampled to death.

As soon as Fricker announced that we were playing British Bulldog, I assumed that this was it: the huge herd of buffalo that was the Camp Fatso kids would stampede over me, leaving nothing but a squished and gory corpse.

'Right,' said Fricker, 'we need our first bulldog.'

I started to walk forward, resigned to my fate.

'Not you, Millicent,' Fricker continued. 'You.' He pointed with the toothbrush at Igor. As the others lined up on the field, Fricker said to me out of the corner of his mouth, 'Don't want you getting too badly hurt this afternoon. Greater things planned for you. Here, help me get this ruddy thing off, would you?'

And so, while carnage took place on the field (most of it enacted by, not upon, Igor), I unscrewed Fricker's toothbrush.

Although I was, obviously, happy about not getting crushed to death, I also felt strangely disappointed in Fricker. Brutal, simple-minded, insane he may have been, but I never thought that he was corrupt. Yet here he was, clearly part of the rotten core of the Camp Fatso establishment, keeping me out of danger so that I could take part in the evening's barbaric entertainment.

8 p.m. The time had come.

Renfrew was coming with me, but I said

goodbye to all my old comrades in Hut Four. Each one knew his role. Each one was prepared to make the ultimate sacrifice to bring down the Evil Empire that was Camp Fatso. I shook them all by the hand. Igor, a tower of strength and a chess genius (I never was to beat him); Dong, inscrutable to the last, but undoubtedly very pleased to meet you; Florian Frost, beetle expert, gentle soul; and, finally, J-Man, my flawed hero. Had he really come good at last, or was he going to betray us all again?

We had a group hug, got slightly embarrassed about it, and then I was off.

The venue was the administration block, where I'd signed in on my first day at Camp Fatso. We were met at the door by a couple of Lardies: hard-faced blimps, smartly dressed in tuxedos and bow-ties, who'd rather crack

your head than a smile.

'What's the vole doing here?' said one,
shoving Renfrew in the chest.

'He's my second.'

'Your what?'

'You know, like in a duel – the guy who helps
the main guy.'

A grunt and we were in. The bouncers led
us past the reception desk, through the room
beyond it, out another door, and down a stairway.
One of the blimps opened a final double door,
and suddenly I was confronted with a space full
of light and noise. There were seats banked up
around a central area, in which I stood. It was
the size of a boxing ring. This probably isn't the
time to bring this up, but why do they call it a
boxing ring when it's square? Anyway, this space
actually *was* round. Or rather, it was an oval. It all

reminded me of the Colosseum, where gladiators and animals fought in Rome. And that was pretty well what this place was about too.

The seats were full. Goons and Lardies, and other people I didn't recognize. Receding chins and braying laughs. Badwig was there, and Boss Skinner, with Gustav on his lap. The loathsome Hercule Paine, looking more like Jabba the Hutt than ever, gave a little tinkling wave with his fingertips.

But pride of place was reserved for the gaunt, sneering figure of Doc Morlock. She was wearing a black gown with a high collar, and looked like a science fiction version of Queen Elizabeth I, crossed with an evil Roman emperor, crossed with a cat's bottom. She was on a sort of throne, and was surrounded by a bodyguard of Lardies.

There was no sign of Mr Fricker, but I didn't have the time or the headspace to work out why. I gave Renfrew a little nod, and he shrank back beyond the inner doorway.

Waiting for me in the ring was Demetrius the Destroyer. He was wearing a wrestler's leotard, in a very stretchy fabric – obviously this was his donut-eating costume. And there, piled up before us, on platters, were the donuts.

Fifty each.

The joy! No, this was beyond joy. It was cosmic. It was the greatest love story in history. It was the coming together of two things that have been searching for each other for all eternity: Dermot Milligan and a platter of fifty donuts.

And I was pleased to see that they were of the plain kind, with just a dusting of icing sugar. There was also a glass of water for each of us,

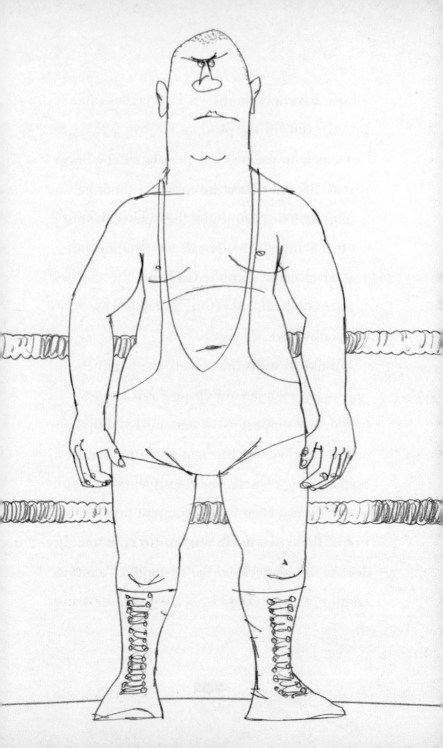

which was considerate.

And vital, for my plan.

Demetrius pointed one massive stubby finger first at me, and then at his mouth. I think he was saying that once he'd eaten the donuts, then he'd eat me. Frankly, I thought he was bluffing, but you never knew with the Lardies.

A trumpet fanfare played, and then Doc Morlock stood.

'I'd like to welcome you all,' she began graciously, 'members of Camp Fatso, family, friends and supporters, to our end-of-camp celebration. We will begin with the traditional donut-eating contest. The rules, for those of you who have not been here before, are simple. The first of these two noble warriors to consume fifty donuts will be declared the champion. Vomiting, fainting, or death from overeating will result in the disqualification of the competitor. Needless to say, the donuts have been prepared using my own virtually fat-free, low-calorie donut mix, which includes ground mung beans and go-go berries, available at all good supermarkets as part of my Dr Morlock range of healthy eating produce.'

Hang on, *healthy* donuts? That was wrong, so wrong. And yet they still looked like donuts, real donuts. Perhaps they'd be OK.

Doc Morlock peered down at me and my mountainous opponent. 'Are you ready?'

The Destroyer and I faced her, and spoke the ancient and noble words:

'We who are about to eat salute you.'

Then Doc Morlock held up a silk scarf. Silence descended. She let the scarf drop. And so began the mightiest donut-eating challenge of my life. Heck, of any life.

Hercule Paine had told me that it had to look like a close-run thing, and I knew at once that matching Demetrius the Destroyer was going to be tricky. I could tell straight away that he was a canny donut eater.

An amateur would have gone off at full speed, cramming the round portions of heaven into his mouth faster than his chops could chew. Result: a serious choking situation. And even if you could get it all down, there was a chance of filling up too quickly. No, the secret of the donut marathon was taking it nice and steady. And that's what Demetrius was doing.

His hand moved slowly but surely, backwards and forwards from the donut platter; three bites and each donut was history, and the process would begin again. No rush, no hurry, just world-class donut eating.

However, you have to remember that I had
been on a starvation diet for nearly two weeks.
So, even though I knew that I should copy the
Destroyer's style, I just couldn't. Like a rank
beginner, I stuffed the first one straight into my
mouth. I didn't even bother to bite: the whole
thing went in. In all the pomp and pageantry
of the occasion I'd forgotten that these were
supposedly healthy donuts. So it was a bit of a
shock when it was actually in my mouth and,
rather than the meltingly lovely sugary explosion
of mouth-bliss, I got a bland ball of stodge, with
a faint aftertaste of bean. But it was still the best
thing I'd eaten in a long time. And, when all's
said and done, a donut is a donut is a donut, and
I was put on this good earth to eat them.

Soon I had got through ten. Demetrius was

on eight. I glanced up and caught the eye of Hercule Paine. He looked a little worried. He'd invested the entire Lardy fortune on this match, and if he lost the bet, then his empire would be wiped out.

I winked. I was letting him know that he and his money were safe. He nodded back. He could probably see what I was doing – building up an early lead to keep things exciting, before falling back later on.

And now I was beginning to get the donut sweats. Fifteen. Sixteen. I paused for breath. The Destroyer, for the first time, began to look a little worried, and upped his pace.

Soon my pile was half finished. I lay back on the floor for a rest. I had the beginnings of an ache in my belly that I knew must eventually emerge as a monstrous burp. As I rested, so

Demetrius sped on. He had gone past me now, into the thirties. Some of the crowd began to jeer – most of them had put their money on me, and they were getting angry.

'Come on, you fat oaf,' someone shouted. Another threw a shoe at me. But my experience of Peruvian shoe-throwing meant that I was able to catch it and toss it back. It was just the spur I needed. I was up again and eating.

Demetrius was looking ill by now. He'd reached forty donuts, and it was his turn to slump back for a break. He emitted a great belch like the mating call of a mastodon in an ancient swamp.

And now I'd got my second wind. I passed his tally at forty-two. But now I felt that there was simply no room left inside me. Every square millimetre was already taken up with donut.

The crowd were growing frantic. They were on their feet. I couldn't pick out individual voices any more: it was just a wall of noise.

OK, it was time for me to get some air out of my system. I burped – not the great vulgar bellowing of the Destroyer, just a normal one, lasting about three seconds. But it was enough. I was back in the game.

Seven to eat. The Destroyer was down to his last three. But he had gone a very strange colour. Something in between green and purple. Grurple, perhaps.

Six left.

Five.

Four.

Three.

We were neck and neck now. The Destroyer was back at the platter. His hand was shaking. His face was crusted with icing sugar and donut crumbs.

Together we ate – donut to donut.

Two left.

Weird lights were flashing in my eyes. Was this the dreaded donut narcosis I'd heard about – a bit like the bends that deep-sea divers suffer from, but caused, not by bubbles of nitrogen in the bloodstream, but by donut molecules furring up the brain arteries?

We were both on our final donut.

The Destroyer sized it up. Moved it towards his mouth, but he was still chewing the remains of the previous three. He staggered and swayed, each stumble greeted with a groan or sigh from the crowd. He belched again, and was clearly on the verge of a major digestive incident.

It was now, with Demetrius swaying before the platter, that I took out the little packet that J-Man had given me. It was one of the sachets of salt occasionally smuggled in to give the gruel some flavour. Salt was banned, so they were rare and valuable. I carefully ripped it open and deliberately stumbled forward to the table. As subtly as I could, I poured the grains into Demetrius's glass of water. No one seemed to notice or care what I was doing – they were too mesmerized by the Destroyer's attempt to get the last donut into his mouth.

He did it. But the claggy mass would not go down. It was then that he reached for his glass of water. He gulped it down in one.

In an instant his face went through a series of violent changes. Happiness, confusion, horror.

Ever gulped salty water? If you have, you know what happens. And it was happening now to the Destroyer.

SPLEEUUUUUUUUURGGGGGGGGH HHHHHHHHHHHHHH!!!!!

The puke spume flew in a high arc, covering Hercule and Boss Skinner and Doc Morlock and many of the other dignitaries. Foul-smelling donut soup was everywhere, in hair and eyes, noses and mouths. Oh yes, the Destroyer sure knew how to vomit. And as everyone knows, it never rains but it pours when it comes to puking. Others in the crowd joined in. One lady puked silently into her handbag. Doc Morlock, her mouth full of vomit, snatched off Badwig's bad wig, and spewed into it. Even Gustav, the horrid sausage dog, joined in, puking violently on Boss Skinner's lap.

The stadium was awash.

It was a vomit bath.

A pukathon.

It was awesome.

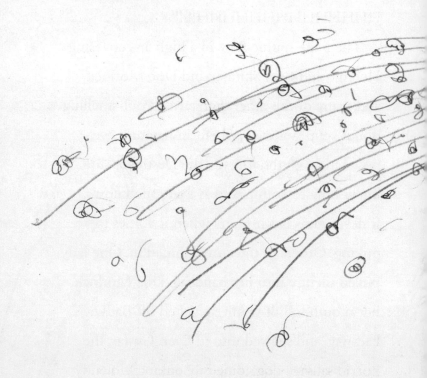

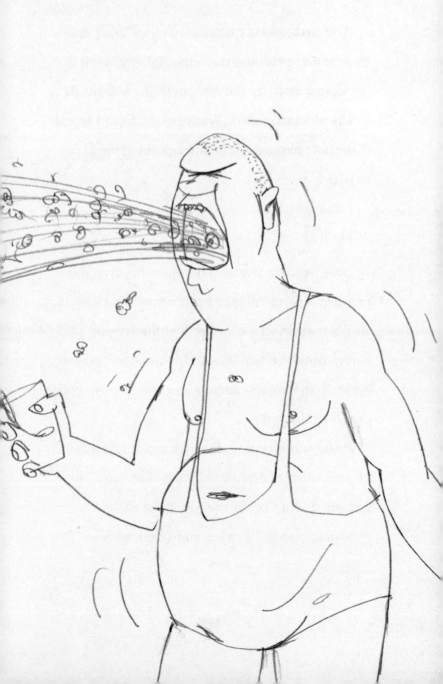

And now it was my time of glory. With one elegant and practised movement, I crammed my last donut into my mouth, chewed, swallowed.

I heard a strangled, 'Nooooooo!' from Hercule Paine, so piercing it cut through the general uproar.

I had won.

He had lost.

Boss Skinner wiped puke from his eyes and grabbed a paintball gun from below his chair. He aimed it at my chest and pulled the trigger. The barrel, however, was blocked with vomit, and it blew up in his face, adding an attractive top coat of red to the puke.

Paine was weeping. Doc Morlock had a look of pure murder on her evil face. 'Get him!' she screamed. 'And bring me my badgers!'

Vomit-covered Lardies and goons moved

towards me, but I was already running.

The endgame was here.

I burst out through the double doors of the puke-pit. Renfrew was poised and ready. He slammed them shut behind me, and then tied the handles together using his belt.

'Won't hold them long,' he said as the doors bent under the force of a hefty Lardy shoulder-barge.

It didn't matter. We were already out of the admin block, moving faster than we'd ever moved before. True, it wasn't actually *that* fast, but you have to remember that Renfrew had very little legs, and I was carrying fifty donuts inside me. But we also had the fate of a camp full of fat kids, plus about a hundred badgers, on our shoulders, so that drove us on.

Of course, there were no goons out on patrol,

and the watchtowers were unmanned, or else we'd have been cut down like poor old Ernesto Gogol.

But I did hear the pounding of heavy feet behind us. Glancing over my shoulder, I saw a group of Lardies coming after us. Somehow they'd got hold of paintball guns. My guess was that the goons had handed them over, and told them to finish us off – they didn't want to get their hands dirty in the actual massacre. A couple of speculative rounds whizzed over our heads, and one splatted on a hut in front of us.

I saw the narrow passage leading to the grim horror of Hut Nineteen. And yes, there, waiting for us, were the reassuring shapes I had come to know so well. They were arranged in a phalanx formation, Spartan style.

J-Man stepped forward. To my delight, I saw

that he was carrying a paintball gun.

'So, the raid on the armoury went well?' I panted.

'As you see. Now, go and do your job, and we will do ours.'

'Just hold them off for as long as you can.'

'They shall not pass.'

I shook his hand, and then shook the hands of the others: Igor, Florian Frost, Dong.

Brave men.

Then I ran through the laser corridor, ignoring the laser detectors. No need to hide or crawl now that the game was afoot.

Behind me I heard the first exchanges: the yells of annoyance and surprise from the Lardies, followed by the first cries of pain. J–Man giving orders.

'Front rank, fire! Second rank, fire!'

I knew that they couldn't hold out for ever against those numbers. They just had to buy me and Renfrew enough time to get away with the badgers.

We didn't bother with the window this time: I just kicked the door down, like a proper action hero (OK, the wood was rotten, but it was still a pretty good feeling).

Inside, I sensed the badgers' excitement immediately. They seemed to know that great (or terrible) things were happening.

As we'd planned, Renfrew pulled away the loose floorboards and opened the trap door while I ran to open the badger cages. On the way, I couldn't resist having a quick look through the window. There were dozens of Lardies lying dazed and splattered across the field, but the Hut Four heroes were being driven steadily back. I saw my guys take hits: the red rounds punching them in the chest, in the arms, in the face. But somehow they still held the narrow passage.

Back to the cages. Some of the beasts were so traumatized that they retreated, terrified of freedom. Others snapped and hissed, unaware that I was their friend, not their tormentor. But most jumped straight out. That encouraged the rest, and soon the hut was a writhing mass of badger.

I went back to the window again. I saw that my men had fallen back through the pass. Their ammo was out – but so, it seemed, was that of the enemy. As I watched I saw the huge figure of Demetrius the Destroyer lumber forward. He was met by Dong, who blocked his way. They wrestled like two great sumo champions. The Destroyer dwarfed Dong, but Dong had the technique, and he threw the bigger man on his back.

But then an even bulkier figure stepped forward – Hercule Paine himself. He calmly took a paintball Luger from inside his jacket, and casually shot Dong between the eyes. The Chinese kid was down and out. But his place was taken by J-Man.

'Don't be a fool,' I heard Paine sneer. 'It's over. You know it's over.'

'I told my friend no one was getting through. You want to try to make me a liar? Bring it on!'

I last saw the two of them grappling together in the narrow pass. But I could not wait for the outcome. I heard the first baying of the hounds: the dogs were coming!

'Come on, Dermot,' Renfrew yelled. 'We've got to get out now, or it's all for nothing.'

'You go first,' I said, this time meaning it as a favour to my little friend, and not out of fear of the dark or spiders or the ghosts of long-dead Italian prisoners. 'I'll follow behind the badgers and drive them on.'

'No,' he replied. 'It's got to be you. If the Lardies get down in the tunnel with us, I'll hold them off. You have to get through to tell the world the truth about Camp Fatso. You've lived it. You tell it.'

There was no time to debate the issue. I nodded and threw myself down the shaft, pushing through the cluster of nervous badgers who were already there, snickering and snapping. I sensed, to my relief, that the others were all coming behind me. Whether they were really following me, Pied Piper style, or just fleeing from the sound of the dreaded sausage dogs, I couldn't say.

I entered the tunnel. It definitely seemed to have shrunk a little since my first reconnaissance mission . . .

Sweating now, heart racing, every nerve on fire, I crawled and crawled and crawled. Had it really been this long before? The badgers were pressing behind me: this was their world, and they sensed freedom and safety ahead, as well as the peril behind. But there was no room for them to squeeze past.

And then suddenly I was at the exit shaft. Exhausted, I heaved myself up the ladder, reached above my head, thrust at the trap door, flung it back. Fresh air. Hope. Salvation.

My head was through. My arms. Then . . . nothing. I shoved, pushed, heaved, but I was stuck fast.

But how? Had the opening somehow narrowed?

No. Of course.

The fifty donuts!

Beneath me I felt the pressure build, heard the sounds of a hundred desperate badgers. OUCH! A sharp nip. They were turning on me! I had to get out or they would tear me apart! Eaten alive by badgers – what a way to go.

I heard a voice from below.

'Dermot, what is it?'

I couldn't get my head down to answer, and didn't want to yell out in case I gave away our position.

And then I sensed movement above me. Two figures emerged from the gloom of the trees.

Goons!

Failure.

It had all been for nothing. I felt strong arms grab me, tug me, lift me. I was out.

And I smelled a strong, familiar smell.

'Pfumpf.'

'Well done, Donut,' said another voice. 'Looks like you pulled it off. The Badger Protection League is for ever in your debt.'

'Ludmilla . . . Tamara . . . what are you doing here?'

'Explain later. We've got to move. These woods are patrolled,' said Tamara.

'Right. But wait – Renfrew.'

I watched the badgers stream out of the escape tunnel, flowing like excited furry water. They were free and safe. I sensed their joy as they capered and danced through the trees.

And then finally Renfrew's head emerged, and Ludmilla lifted him out, as easily as you'd lift your pet hamster out of its cage.

But elsewhere in the woods I heard the sounds of pursuit. Goons shouting, dogs yapping.

We ran blindly through the trees, with the thick undergrowth tearing at our clothes. Finally we made it to the road.

'If we get to the village we'll be safe,' said
Tamara. 'We can call the police from there.'

And then I saw the lights of an approaching car.

'Flag it down,' said Renfrew. 'We can get a lift.'

Ludmilla stepped out into the middle of the

road like a huge iron robot. The car stopped.

'Get in,' said a voice.

We piled into the back seats, our relief gushing out as breathless laughter. The car felt safe. Outside I saw the beams of torches cutting through the trees. The car started moving. I looked at the hands on the steering wheel. They were clothed in black gloves. But there was something unnatural about the flesh beneath.

Something . . . artificial.

The driver turned slowly towards us. And there I saw the grimly smiling face of Mr Fricker.

Saturday 14 April

'FRICKER!' squeaked Spam. 'No way!'

'F-f-f-f-f-flipping h-h-h-heck,' said Corky, whose stammer was definitely improving.

'I don't get it,' said Spam. 'If you got nabbed by Fricker, how come you're here and not, like, dog meat or something?'

We were sitting on the wall by the canal. It was the usual gang: Spam, Renfrew, Corky and Jim. And me, of course. I'd been telling the story, while Renfrew sat quietly, an enigmatic smile on his face. Well, the enigmatic smile alternated with bulging cheeks as he ate one of the donuts I'd bought for everyone.

'Don't you get it? He was a member of the Badger Protection League. He just infiltrated Camp Fatso to help rescue them. He knew where the tunnel came out, and arranged for Tamara and Ludmilla to be there when we emerged. He's a bit like Q in James Bond.'

'Oh, cool,' said Spam. 'So, he's a goody, after all? Who'd have thought it?'

'The world's a complicated place, Spam,' I said. 'It's possible that the same person can be a goody and a baddy, depending on . . . stuff . . . er . . . circumstances.'

'But what happened next?' asked Spam. 'I mean, with the camp, and your friends, J-Man and the others?'

'Oh, as soon as we raised the alarm the security forces went in there and liberated the place – but not before J-Man and the rest of the Hut Four guys managed to break into Hut One and liberated all the crisps and chocolate the Lardies had stashed there. J-Man texted me just after he got out – he said kids were wandering around with chocolate all over their faces, hallucinating on their sugar-and-salt highs, and the Lardies could do nothing about it. The camp's been closed down now. They'll never be able to torture kids with gruel again. And the badgers are safe.'

'What about Doc Morlock?'

'I heard she escaped. But somehow I don't think we've seen the last of her.'

'What a load of old rubbish,' laughed Jim, who's known me much longer than the others.

'You might fool these guys, but I know what you're like, Dermot. You're just making it all up. You had a boring two weeks in fat camp and thought you'd turn it into one of your stories. I mean, badgers . . . goons . . . guns . . . electric fences . . . it's a joke. Come on, tell us, Renfrew – it's all a load of claptrap, isn't it?'

Renfrew shrugged and pointed to his full mouth, indicating that he couldn't speak. The others all took that as an admission that we'd invented the story. I wasn't going to protest. Sometimes the more you go on about something, particularly if it's about what a hero you are, and how you've saved loads of badgers from a terrible fate, the less people are inclined to believe you.

And then I saw a group of girls walking towards us along the path by the canal. It was

Tamara Bello with the posse of scary girls who'd been there for the toenail incident, which now felt like about a hundred years ago. Ludmilla was with them as well. It looked like they'd given her a bit of a makeover. She looked quite nice in her pfumpfish way.

I got ready for an unpleasant combination of being ignored and insulted.

Instead, Tamara came up to me. She was eating a packet of crisps. She held out the bag, right there, in front of her girls and my guys.

'Want one?'

'Huh? Oh, what flavour?'

She looked at me for a moment, a half-smile on her lips.

'Badger.'

DONUT COUNT:

I gave all my donuts to the guys. After the fifty I ate yesterday, even the donut-eating champion of Camp Fatso needs a day off.

Acknowledgements

My thanks to the amazing team at Random House Children's Books, in particular Kelly Hurst, Natalie Doherty, Sophie Nelson, Jessica Clarke, Lauren Bennett and Harriet Venn.

And a very special thanks to Ngawara Madeleine Madison, who found my lost iPad, which contained the first draft of this book.

HAVE YOU READ DERMOT'S OTHER DONUT DIARIES?

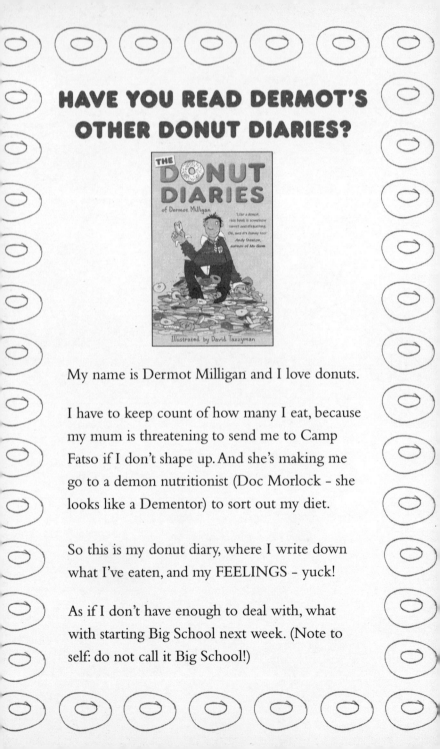

THE DONUT DIARIES
of Dermot Milligan

'Like a donut, this book is somehow sweet and disgusting. Oh, and it's funny too!'
Andy Stanton, author of Mr Gum

Illustrated by David Tazzyman

My name is Dermot Milligan and I love donuts.

I have to keep count of how many I eat, because my mum is threatening to send me to Camp Fatso if I don't shape up. And she's making me go to a demon nutritionist (Doc Morlock - she looks like a Dementor) to sort out my diet.

So this is my donut diary, where I write down what I've eaten, and my FEELINGS - yuck!

As if I don't have enough to deal with, what with starting Big School next week. (Note to self: do not call it Big School!)

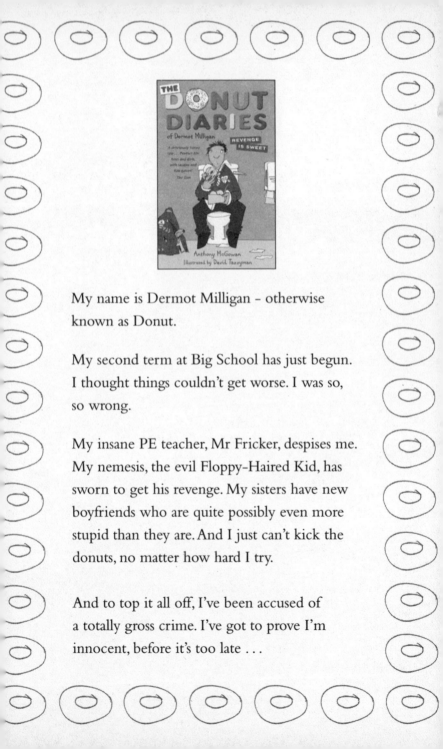

My name is Dermot Milligan – otherwise
known as Donut.

My second term at Big School has just begun.
I thought things couldn't get worse. I was so,
so wrong.

My insane PE teacher, Mr Fricker, despises me.
My nemesis, the evil Floppy-Haired Kid, has
sworn to get his revenge. My sisters have new
boyfriends who are quite possibly even more
stupid than they are. And I just can't kick the
donuts, no matter how hard I try.

And to top it all off, I've been accused of
a totally gross crime. I've got to prove I'm
innocent, before it's too late . . .

I ♥ donuts

I
♡
donuts